THE WORLD'S FATE ARRIVED LIKE A SHOOTING STAR,
A RARE GIFT CALLING FOR COURAGE

MAGIC OF THE
LOST CRYSTAL

AMBER

NewDelhi • London

BLUEROSE PUBLISHERS
India | U.K.

Copyright © **Amber** 2025

All rights reserved by author. No part of this publication may be reproduced, stored in a retrieval system or transmitted in any form or by any means, electronic, mechanical, photocopying, recording or otherwise, without the prior permission of the author. Although every precaution has been taken to verify the accuracy of the information contained herein, the publisher assumes no responsibility for any errors or omissions. No liability is assumed for damages that may result from the use of information contained within.

BlueRose Publishers takes no responsibility for any damages, losses, or liabilities that may arise from the use or misuse of the information, products, or services provided in this publication.

For permissions requests or inquiries regarding this publication, please contact:

BLUEROSE PUBLISHERS
www.BlueRoseONE.com
info@bluerosepublishers.com
+91 8882 898 898
+4407342408967

ISBN: 978-93-6783-344-5

Cover Design: Shubham
Typesetting: Sagar

First Edition: January 2025

*"When you hear the call of adventure,
make sure HOPE catches you first."*

*A gripping tale of adventure, bravery, and unyielding
courage, where the fate of the world rests in
the hands of a daring young girl.*

Contents

Prologue	1
Chapter 1 Veil of Time	5
Chapter 2 Ella's Escape	8
Chapter 3 Ella's Secrets	10
Chapter 4 The Devourer of Fear	13
Chapter 5 Reason Unveiled	14
Chapter 6 Risk or Failure	17
Chapter 7 The African Visit	18
Chapter 8 The Spellbound Dream	21
Chapter 9 Devil's Eye	22
Chapter 10 Beyond the Fear	26
Chapter 11 Mystics of Indonesia	31
Chapter 12 Breeze of Freedom	34
Chapter 13 Heart of Indonesia	37
Chapter 14 The Chasm	39
Chapter 15 The Hidden Kingdom	42
Chapter 16 Fangs Below	44
Chapter 17 Deep in the Ocean	47
Chapter 18 Queen of Water	50
Chapter 19 Shimmering Depths	52
Chapter 20 Mysterious Caves	55
Chapter 21 The Water creature	58
Chapter 22 The Water Waves	60
Chapter 23 The Magical Video	63
Chapter 24 The Lost Awakened	65

Chapter 25 Under the Spanish Sky	70
Chapter 26 Echoes of Flamenco	75
Chapter 27 Sapphire's POV	77
Chapter 28 Back to Enid's POV	79
Chapter 29 Payback	81
Chapter 30 Fountain of Life	83
Chapter 31 Under the Moonlight	86
Chapter 32 Serenity of Greece	88
Chapter 33 The Scarlet Beast	91
Chapter 34 Sapphire's POV (Part 2)	93
Chapter 35 Determination	95
Chapter 36 The Saviour Flowers	99
Chapter 37 End of the Beginning	102
Chapter 38 Magic in My Veins	107
Chapter 39 Ella's POV	112
Chapter 40 The Beast Unleashed	114
Chapter 41 Enid vs Drogeler	118
Chapter 42 The Young Girl	121
Chapter 43 Ella's Memories	123
Chapter 44 Enid's Memories	128
Chapter 45 Beginning of the End	130
Chapter 46 Possession	133
Chapter 47 The Worthy Holder	136
Chapter 48 Triumph of Peace	140
Chapter 49 Reunion	142
Chapter 50 Moments of Bliss	145
Quotes	149
Which Symbol Do You Represent?	151

Prologue

About two thousand years ago, a kingdom was oppressed by fear, due to the reign of an evil sorceress named Ronia. Her ways were cruel and wicked. The civilians knew they could not endure Ronia's reign much longer, but none dared to challenge her as nothing, but innocent lives would be lost by doing so. They all lived under the cloud of fear, knowing freedom was impossible. They knew all their protests would go in vain, so they did none.

However, a brave young girl lived with completely different dreams. She believed in the freedom of her kingdom and saw the visions of everyone being free and happy. She stated that nothing is impossible until you think so. Despite her youth and the sorceress's immense power, the girl resolved to stand against Ronia. Her fellow civilians tried to dissuade her, calling it a foolish and reckless decision, but she didn't let fear cloud her dreams away.

With a heart full of courage, the girl set out alone to confront the sorceress, determined to bring an end to Ronia's tyranny. The girl was no match for the powerful sorceress and when she confronted Ronia, she got captured. The girl would now be shattered in no time.

Suddenly, the little young girl was filled with immense powers. Her bravery, kindness, courage, and powerful dreams of seeking freedom were all the qualities of a true power keeper. She was then gifted with powers that only the strongest could dream of. Ronia was stunned at this sight but still believed she was the strongest of all. Her overconfidence got the better of her. The girl blasted Ronia using her new powers, leaving Ronia speechless. The girl's hope had lifted the heavy cloud of fear which had lasted for ages over her kingdom. Yet, she was unaware of the unforeseen twist.

Ronia didn't want to die in vain. She wanted to leave a mark of evil. So, with her dying embers and hatred, she created the world's strongest poison and knew its effect was everlasting. Using that she poisoned the young girl. The girl didn't spot this coming and soon she was in the last phase of her life. She knew that there was a need for someone to help the world in times of danger.

She transferred her powers into an ordinary rock making it a shimmering, ruby-red crystal blazing with extraordinary powers. Using her remaining embers, she hid the crystal in a safe place so that only the worthy holder could get his hands on it. The girl had changed her kingdom's fate with her priceless hope. The civilians recognized the signs of freedom and rejoiced. They respected the young girl's sacrifice above everything else and decided to pass on this story from generation to generation.

Within time, her identity was lost however her deeds were still alive. Within time, the crystal further broke into ten pieces, each with a symbol representing a different kind of power. After that, the crystals were never to be seen again unless the world was in crisis.

Like every story, this episode became a legend -"The Legend of the Lost Crystal."

Chapter 1

Veil of Time

'The village, where the battle of Ronia and the young girl took place is now a part of Milan, Italy.' The place where we live. Cool coincidence, isn't it? The story ends here, Enid." said my mother, after finishing the story. She then closed the storybook and placed it back on the shelf.

"Mom, do you believe in this legend?" I asked.

"Well, people sometimes make the stories from their fantasy, but sometimes they can be real too." She winked.

"That's interesting, Mom. I'll now go to sleep."

I went to bed, wondering if the story was real or not. I was only four then, so I forgot about it later. But as I've grown up, I know it was just a legend. There are legends of fairies who come from clouds and hobgoblins who burst out of the volcanoes. But none of it is true. So, this one isn't true either. It was just a fairytale.

Back to the present, I was getting ready for school. Today is my first day in my new grade. I only have one friend and 100 bullies at school. Yup! That's the place where I'm headed. It's not like my school days are bad or something. They're great actually. Only when those bullies don't interrupt in between.

Anyway, I got ready and left my room to have the best waffles and cream in the world, freshly cooked by my 'madre' (Italian word for mom). Then, I had some morning gossip with her (that's one of my favourite hobbies) and left for school.

I live in Milan, but it's not just a city for me, it's my home. Sometimes it feels like it has its own soul as it enriches people's joy and helps them cherish their happiness. You know, I haven't been on an international vacation, but I don't complain because I love how Milan's every corner feels alive with culture and character. Milan's streets mix history and style, with cobblestone alleys, elegant buildings, and modern avenues. Trams glide past luxury boutiques, cozy cafés, and historic landmarks like the Duomo. The best part is the 'Milan Fashion Week'. I visit that every year and it's just extraordinary, showcasing world-class talent and creativity.

Every day, on my way to school, I wave to people I meet. Courtesy you know. As I was wondering about Milan and waving at people, I realized that I was getting late for school. So, I had to run a little bit. I get distracted very easily. Just like usual, Ella reached before me, my only friend.

"Late again? Huh?" said Ella.

"As usual.", I said, shrugging my shoulders.

We then headed to the school building. My school is not so far from my house, but I'm always late (even when I wake up early in the morning).

"I think I didn't bring my chemistry homework.", Ella said, as we were heading to the locker room.

"Umm-You're holding it, Ella.", I said, pointing to the folder in her hand.

Ella looked down and saw herself holding the homework.

"Oops! Silly me."

We giggled softly. We reached the locker room by then and started to take out our stuff.

"You're lookin' forward to the chemistry class? A new lesson today.", I asked.

"No!" she exclaimed. "Who'll be excited for that class? No one wants their faces blasted off."

Face blasted off? How can she say that? Chemistry is her favorite. What's going on with her? Although I didn't mention it initially, I sensed something off with her. When I met her today in the morning, she didn't have the energy she always does. She's my best friend, so I know. Can't hide anything from me.

Chapter 2

Ella's Escape

"Oh! I-I-I forgot something in my locker. I'll go get it. Be back in a few minutes." Ella stammered.

I looked at her with confusion. We just came from the lockers to our classroom. She is definitely up to something, and I'll find out what it is.

"Ella, I also need to grab something. Let's go together."

Her expression said it all; she didn't want me tagging along. Why? And if you're wondering- What if she's planning a surprise for me, that's why she's acting this way. So, no. First, my birthday was last month so there's no special occasion. Second, she would've acted funny. Not suspicious like she has done a crime.

"Something wrong, El?" I asked, concerned.

"No, everything's fine.", she replied quickly.

We then headed to the locker room. Ella pulled something out of her locker that wasn't stationary or school-related and definitely not surprise-related. It was a weird-shaped bottle. I hadn't seen such a thing before. It was made of glass and had some carvings on it. Inside the bottle, was a lilac-coloured liquid.

I asked, "What is that?"

"I can't tell you.", she replied in her low voice.

"Why? We tell each other everything!" I protested.

Ella looked at me with a strange intensity in her eyes. Instead of answering my question, she said, "We'll see each other only if I fail."

"Only if you fail? Fail at what?" I exclaimed in utter shock.

"At destroying the world.", she said in a low voice with the same strange intensity in her eyes.

I froze, my mind racing. Meet again, fail, destroy the world? What on earth was she talking about? Has she participated in a drama act for school and she's practicing it? I hope so.

"Good act, Ella." I forced a laugh. "I didn't know you could do acting so well. You'll do great in your school drama." I continued, with confusing expressions on my face.

"It's not an act my dear. It's reality. Face it." After a pause, she said, "Well, you're still in shock. I'll leave. No time to watch you. I got work to do.", she said as I was still blinking my eyes rapidly, and my jaw dropped to the floor. Then, I realized she was being for real, so I regained myself and without fully understanding the situation, I stepped closer.

"Are you for real? You're not going anywhere."

"Too late, Enid. You spent too much time blinking."

With that, she raised the bottle in her hand, drank the liquid, and in an instant, she vanished.

Chapter 3
Ella's Secrets

I couldn't believe my eyes. She vanished into thin air the moment she drank from that mysterious bottle. How's that possible? I'm still trying to think that this is for the school act. But, it really happened. It's not an act. And the way she spoke, it was like she was the star of an action film. Or perhaps the villain. But here's the thing- she should know better; Life isn't some action flick.

I had to find Ella, and the first place that came to mind was her house. I need answers and they'd be there or at least a clue to where she'd gone. I quickly packed my backpack and was just about to head out when something caught my eye.

On the floor, right where she had vanished, lay an old, dusty book. She dropped it in her hurry to disappear. Curious, I picked it up and flipped open the cover. My heart skipped a beat as I read the title: The Legend of the Lost Crystal.

It was the same story my mom used to tell me when I was a kid, about a mysterious crystal with powers beyond imagination. Why did she have this? Did she start reading kids' storybooks again? I thumbed through the pages and realized this wasn't like my book's version. Ella's copy was full of handwritten notes, strange symbols, and pages that seemed... well, alive.

What on earth was she up to? What does it have to do with this legend? What if it's- no it can't be. Ugh! I don't have time to dwell on deciphering the symbols and notes and the mystery she has left me with of 'destroying the world'. I need to find Ella, fast. I got up and left the school building, sprinting to her house. Thanks to my running skills, I reached her house in a few minutes. I stood at her front door and knocked, panting.

"Ella? Mrs. Rossi? Are you in there?" I said, taking huge breaths.

Ella's mom opened the door, eyeing me with concern. "Oh, Enid! You look worn out. Were you running?"

"Uh, yeah! My teacher needed my notebook, and Ella left it in her room, so I just came by to grab it." I said, gulping for air. I wasn't sure if she bought my excuse, but it had to do.

Ella's mom said, "I always remind Ella to return everyone's belongings on time. But what can we do? She forgets every time."

"It's alright.", I said while trying to catch my breath.

Ella's mom stepped aside, allowing me in, and I wasted no time. I hurried down the hall, ascended the stairs, and barged the door open to Ella's room. Ella wasn't there but what I found left me stunned.

Her room was a chaotic mess, nothing like the tidy space I'd seen before. The lights were shattered, pages were scattered across the floor, and ink stains marked every surface.

I spotted two more bottles of that strange liquid that she had drank at school. And there were massive books, nearly as wide as me. It looked like her whole life had been thrown into chaos and I couldn't shake the feeling that something was very wrong.

Moreover, when did she even start reading this much? Probably around the time she decided on this 'destroy-the-world' idea of hers.

I looked around and saw another book, titled as: The Devourer of Fear

Chapter 4
The Devourer of Fear

"After the incident involving Ronia and the young girl, a monster called Drogeler was born. He fed on the fear of people- a creature of pure horror and menace. Drogeler hid beneath the floors, lying there in wait to collect the fear and grow stronger with each shiver and gasp. His plan was simple: when he would be powerful enough, he would strike, leaving no one prepared for the horror he would unleash.

Many powerful magicians, sorcerers, and wizards rose to challenge Drogeler, each determined to defeat him. But one by one, they failed; their efforts fell short of the power needed to destroy him. What they didn't know was his hidden secret- the truth known only to Drogeler.

Once, he had been human. But through dark magic, he transformed himself into a creature that thrived on fear. Then, unexpectedly, a miracle happened. Ten jewels, fragments of the ruby-red crystal, one of the most powerful magical artifacts on earth, appeared from distant parts of the world. They reunited in a hidden cave, and together, they held a power strong enough to banish Drogeler.

He was cast deep into the Japan Trench, sealing his fright away beneath the waves. The very crystals which have banished Drogeler, are the crystals which will bring him back..."

Chapter 5
Reason Unveiled

Drogeler- could he be the reason Ella is so desperate to find the crystals? A chilling thought crept into my mind: the liquid Ella drank wasn't just any concoction; it was a potion. Not just any potion, but a teleportation potion.

But wait! How am I supposed to stop her? Maybe the better question is—am I even supposed to stop her? Do I even have the strength or the means to do it? What if I fail? What if this isn't my fight at all? Maybe someone else is meant to handle this. Someone stronger, wiser... someone who actually knows what they're doing.

But then again, who else even knows? Who else has seen what I've seen? If I tell anyone, they'll probably just think I'm crazy. If I walk away now, would that mean I'm abandoning everyone who's depending on me, even if they don't know it yet?

So, in the end, it's all up to me. I took a deep breath, steadying myself. I knew what Ella was planning, but I had no idea where she was. She must have a secret lair. Every villain has one, right? No, Enid! This isn't some movie. Get a grip. Come back to reality. Pacing back and forth in her room, panicked and clueless, my eyes landed on a piece of paper.

Scribbled across it, were the words: The locations of the lost crystal pieces. With my heart racing, I flipped the paper over. There was a list of countries where, I suppose, the crystals are.

How on earth am I supposed to get there? By ship? No way. By air? Not a chance. By car? That's not exactly ocean-friendly travel. Then, the two bottles of the teleportation potions caught my eye. I hope it doesn't cause side effects. I'm not keen at all to drink this thing but this is the only budget-friendly option available to me.

I took a deep breath, feeling the weight of what lay ahead. This was so much bigger than I'd ever imagined.

Bracing myself, I began to pack the essentials. Potions, the list, the two books, my pocket money, a small first aid kit, phone, charger, water, and snacks- but snacks are in Ella's mom's kitchen. I went downstairs and saw Mrs. Rossi watching TV. Good opportunity. I moved forward, tiptoeing carefully. Then I reached the kitchen slab, bent down, and crawled over to the pantry.

I slowly opened it and grabbed some chips, biscuits, and a noodle packet. That should be enough. I closed the door quietly and started to crawl the way out. But, as I turned, I froze as Mrs. Rossi was standing in front of me. A low scream escaped me.

"Enid, why are you on the floor?" Mrs. Rossi asked, eyeing me with suspicion.

I forced a laugh and said, "Umm- I slipped and fell. Clumsy me."

"Are you alright?", she asked, still looking at me suspiciously.

"I'm perfectly fine. I better leave now. Bye." I said quickly.

"But- Enid-"

Before Mrs. Rossi could say anything more, I picked up Ella's skateboard and dashed away. Phew! That was a close call.

Chapter 6
Risk or Failure

I ran down the lane to my house, stopping just before the door. I thought, pausing to let the reality of this journey sink in. This adventure held more risk than I could imagine. I was leaving home with no guarantee I'd return and no promise I'd ever see my mother again. I had no idea what I'd face out there. I still can't believe that the crystals actually exist or that Ella really disappeared using a magical concoction. I thought these things existed in fiction movies. But it's all true now.

And if I didn't go, everything would fall apart. According to how dangerous Drogeler is (if he exists) and what Ella is planning to do, people wouldn't be together and safe like they are today. It's all up to me. All of this is hard to grasp. Everyone's happiness depends on my success.

I have to stop Ella from destroying the world. Deep down, I know she isn't the type to shatter everyone's joy. I quickly wrote a letter to my mom, hoping it would ease her worry. I don't know if she'll believe me or not, but it'll have to do. With a deep breath, I grabbed my backpack and took out the potion. Steeling myself, I opened the lid and drank it, forcing myself to stay calm.

In an instant, I was in South Africa.

Chapter 7

The African Visit

I struggled to open my eyes, as the sunlight was falling straight. When I finally managed to open them, I realized that I was really in South Africa. I gasped. For minutes, I was just blinking my eyes, letting the reality sink in. Then, I braced myself and looked around to figure out in which city I was. I wandered until I stumbled upon a sign that read, 'Devil's Peak, Cape Town'. Alright then! Cape Town it is. But the question arises- How do I find where the crystal is?

Cape Town is not a small city. I've no idea what to do. It is all so complicated. I'm not in Italy. I never even left Milan. Now, I'm miles away from my home with no idea what to do. Only one thought flashed in my mind. Ella's book; the Legend of the Lost Crystal. It had some symbols which weren't in my copy. Maybe, it'll have some information or clue.

I started to look for an abandoned street to read the book peacefully. I know! Risky it is. But had no choice. I sat down and flipped through the pages of the book. There were ten symbols drawn in one of the pages. I opened Google Lens and scanned the symbols.

Google went blank. How can Google go blank? It seriously doesn't know about the symbols! If Google doesn't know, then who does?

Sad and disappointed, I just sank into a corner. I had no idea what they meant and no idea how to find the crystals in this big country; I was no symbol decoder. I had no one with me, except for this little stuff bird (I saw it lying beside me when I turned around in distress). This wasn't before; what is this doing here? Seeing me all confused, I suppose.

"Chi- chi- chi."

I jumped from my seat in horror. What on earth just happened? Did I hear the stuff bird chirp? I gazed at the bird. It was a toy; how can it chirp? Perhaps, it's my imagination. I'm just hallucinating, due to my stress.

I closed my eyes to think of something to find the first crystal. When I opened them again, I saw the same bird flying in front of me. I was stunned; a bombshell dropped on me. How's that possible? How had it become real?

I stood up, as it continued chirping, to go and find some better place where toys don't become real. As I started to leave, I felt like it wanted to say something to me. I was pretty confused. Still, I decided to ask her. But before that, I looked around to see if there were any people because if someone sees me talking to a bird, they'll think I'm a raving lunatic.

"Are you trying to say something to me?", I asked, still thinking why I was doing so.

"Uh yes! It's about time you understood." said the bird.

I stumbled backward, my heart pounding with shock and horror. My mind refused to process what I was hearing—it was speaking to me. How's this possible? After Ella's disappearance episode, everything going on around me is bizarre. Everything is proving science wrong.

"What? You can't believe it? Better believe it then. And by the way-" The bird was saying something to me, but I was too dumbstruck to listen to it.

"Enid! Back to earth. Don't be scared. You can trust me. I'm here to help you.", she said.

"How do you know my name and how exactly will you help?" I questioned her, still in disbelief.

"If I tell you how to find the crystal, you'll trust me right?" asked the bird.

"Not so easily. What if you're on the side of Ella and Drogeler, and you're here to distract me."

"I expected that answer. It's wise not to trust easily because trust must be earned. I'm a magical bird. I'll gain your trust."

Saying that she started to circle my head, her feathers shimmering in the sunlight. She circled around me a few times, leaving a trail of shimmering sparkles. Before I knew it, I found myself drifting off to sleep.

Chapter 8

The Spellbound Dream

I realized that the bird had put me into an enchanted sleep. I was in a magical dream. I don't know what she's up to, so I gotta find it out. I walked for a few meters and saw a girl, captured by a sorceress. Was that Ronia and girl captured, the young girl mentioned in the story?

I wasn't sure. So I moved closer and became sure when the girl suddenly transformed into a powerful sorceress. Now, I was able to witness every detail of what happened in the story.

However, the story never revealed how she defeated Ronia; that was the crucial knowledge I needed. The ten symbols crafted in Ella's book were present in Ronia's castle. Using her power, the girl gathered all the symbols from Ronia's fortress, and they began to accumulate Ronia's magic.

Ronia couldn't stop this process; she was on the brink of death, her magic all depleted. In a desperate move, she transformed her hatred into poison, and the girl was soon affected by it. She then did what she needed to do. She formed the broken crystal and divided it into two pieces. The exact scene from the story unfolded before me.

Each piece contained five symbols, which explained why they were further divided into ten pieces. In a dazzling display, the ten crystals, along with their symbols, soared into the air, leaving only the remnants of Ronia behind. I stood there, astonished and speechless.

Chapter 9

Devil's Eye

I woke up, stunned as well as determined, to find the crystal. But, this doesn't prove that this bird is innocent.

"Well! I still can't trust you. Even Ella could've shown me the dream. Not convincing enough."

"I knew you would say that. That's why I've another proof prepared." She said.

"And what's that?" I questioned.

"You've got the grimoire with you? Don't you?", she spoke.

"Umm- Are you talking about the book I've got? How do you know that?", I asked, stunned.

"Yes. That book is actually a 'Grimoire'. I know you've it as I can sense its presence. I'm not an ordinary bird." She paused and continued, "Flip to page 2034."

I did as she said. When I came to the page. There was an image of this bird. Under it said- **Sapphire. The one who** I couldn't read as the lines were smudged so I then read the bottom part- **She remains the only one who knows the symbols and the riddles to find the lost crystal since the crystals broke into pieces.**

In the era of Drogeler, she summoned the crystals to end his reign but also revealed their current location to him. As she grew weak, she couldn't change the locations. Yet, she only answers to- And then there was another line smudged. I read the line afterward- **She's there to guide the person who embarks on the journey to find the crystals for the greater good.**

WOAH! That's my reaction after reading this paragraph.

I asked, "Well! How can I know you're the Sapphire bird, not a disguised one?"

"Now, flip to the next page.", she said, playfully.

I flipped and there were some carvings made on it. The bird then stepped on that page and the book started glowing. It seemed alive. It sure was an amazing sight. After a few seconds, it stopped shimmering, and the book started to write something... by itself?! That was so cool.

It wrote- **Hello Sapphire. Long time no see.**

What?! Did the book recognize her?

The bird said, "Well, I suppose, you can trust me a little bit? Because now you should. I've provided you enough proof and anyway the grimoire never lies. The magic never lies."

She emphasized the last line. I guess she can be trusted.

"Okay. Congrats! You gained my trust. So, can you tell me where the first crystal is?"

"Where the symbol lies.", she answered.

What an abrupt answer!

"Where does it lie? That's what I'm asking.", I asked again.

"I guess you didn't the grimoire's words carefully. It said-symbols and riddles. I'll tell you how it works. Because of the magic drifting away, I don't remember where it exactly lies. I remember the riddles and the clues I left for the search of the crystals before Drogeler."

I sighed and said, "Okay then! You tell me the riddle you've got."

"It's somewhere in Devil's Peak. The riddle is LIES BENEATH THE MEMORY, ALONG WITH A DEVIL'S EYE."

I exclaimed, "Seriously! What a riddle! You could've made an easier one. Anyways, I'll try to solve it."

"Well. Riddles aren't easy.", she answered joyfully and turned around to play with a cat, that was roaming there. Great! She'll only tell me the riddle and I'll take all the tension to solve it, zooming my brain to its fullest. Alas! I sighed and tried to solve it.

It says that 'a memory lies'. But, of whom? And what is meant by the 'Devil's eye'? Wait! I've seen something like that before. That's when it hit me. The symbols from Ella's book! Or I should say – the grimoire. I quickly grabbed it and started to flip the pages. There it was: A symbol of a devil's eye. Ronia's eye. I had seen this in that magical dream as well.

Now, I just needed to figure out what was meant by 'memory'. Maybe if I roamed around the city, something would click. I headed out with Sapphire, keeping my eyes open, scanning every detail around us. Then, I spotted a sign: Rhodes Memorial, Devil's Peak. Suddenly, it made sense.

The memory referred to the memorial of Cecil John Rhodes, the South African politician. The crystal must be there. I made my way to the site, but it was crowded. I'd have to wait until nightfall to get a closer look.

Chapter 10

Beyond the Fear

As night fell, I sat behind some boulders, staring at the memorial. I had no idea how I'd get close enough to find the crystal. The area was packed with security.

"Uh, Sapphire, any idea how I'm supposed to grab the crystal?" I whispered.

"What an amazing question! Didn't I already help you figure out where it is? What else do you want me to do?" She quipped, eating my snacks.

"Something that doesn't involve eating my chips!" I sighed.

"Oh Baby Girl! Oh, Little Enid! This is your first time on an adventure like this. All I can say is, that you should-" She paused.

I asked, "I should?"

"FIGHT LIKE A NINJA! And let me eat those chips.", she said.

"What?! Huh?! Fight? Ninja? You want me to fight those big guys? They'll throw me to Milan in a second." I gasped.

"Oh! Don't be silly. Maybe, you can trade the crystal with your chips.", she said, casually.

"Birdie, things don't work like that here." I told her.

"Then, I don't know further. Figure it out yourself."

It seemed this bird would only help me this much. The rest, I'd have to figure out on my own. She does have a good job; only tells riddles and clues.

I took a deep breath, gathered my thoughts, and focused on how I could reach the crystal. I needed a plan. Around the memorial statue, there were four guards in total: two stationed at the south gateway and two at the north.

But the north gateway had one advantage: a manhole nearby that I could slip through to access the memorial grounds. It wasn't exactly the most legal approach, but I didn't have a choice. I saw Sapphire sleeping peacefully. I had to tell her that I was leaving for the crystal, but she was asleep.

I held her gently and placed her in my backpack. I rushed toward the other manhole, the one outside the memorial, determined to reach the one inside. With a deep breath, I lifted the cover and climbed down, my heart racing with urgency.

The moment I entered, a horrible smell hit me like a wall. It was awful—thick, sour, and nearly impossible to ignore. My stomach turned, but I knew I couldn't let it stop me. I quickly pinched my nose shut, trying not to breathe too deeply and pressing forward.

The tunnel was dark and damp, and my heart pounded louder with each step. I ran as fast as I could, my footsteps echoing in the silence.

Finally, I reached the manhole inside the memorial area. Gripping the ladder tightly, I climbed up carefully, my hands trembling slightly with the effort. At the top, I paused to listen, making sure the area above was clear. Then, ever so slowly, I lifted the heavy lid, inch by inch, taking care not to let it scrape or clang.

Once I was sure it was safe, I pushed myself up through the opening and slipped out as quietly as possible. Every movement felt tense and deliberate as I stayed low, avoiding any sudden noise or movement that might draw attention. The cool night air brushed against my face, but I couldn't relax just yet.

Keeping to the shadows, I moved quickly but silently, darting inside to stay out of the guards' sight. Phew! Two guards were already taken care of, but I wasn't done yet. Four more to go. This was only the beginning.

I tiptoed over to some nearby bushes, crouching low and trying to stay invisible. Now, the real question was: How on earth was I going to distract the guards near the Rhodes statue?

It felt nearly impossible, and I didn't exactly have a list of brilliant ideas. I racked my brain, thinking back to every action film I'd ever seen. Whenever someone needed to distract the security, they usually threw something like a rock or anything in the opposite direction to create a diversion. It seemed like a decent idea, but will it work?

But what if I throw a rock and the guards are too smart?

They might figure out someone tossed it from the opposite side, and then bam! My plan would backfire. Backfire wait, Sapphire! She could help me.

The question was whether she'd even listen to me. I shook her awake gently.

"Listen, birdie, I need a favor."

She blinked at me groggily. "Ugh, Enid, you woke me from a perfectly peaceful sleep... a favor? What now?"

"I want you to fly to the other side and hit the guards with some pebbles.", I said.

"Then, what'll you do?" asked Sapphire.

"Afterwards, I'll grab the crystal, and we'll leave for our next stop."

"Sounds good. I'm in."

Sapphire flew to the other side and started throwing rocks at the guards. They all were startled. Two of them went to check who was doing that.

But the other two remained there. How'll I distract them? Then I remembered Sapphire's words: FIGHT LIKE A NINJA! I knew what I had to do. I couldn't sit back, paralysed by fear; I had to face those guys. With courage, I marched towards them. I just hope I don't mess it up. One of them spotted me running but, I wasn't scared.

The guard shouted "This little girl! She is doing all this. We'll have to report her."

I leaped and struck the guard, making him land on the ground.

The next one rushed towards me. The guard I knocked out earlier, dropped his lamp and I rolled it. The other one tripped, crashing into his fallen partner. With the two guards down, I knew I had to act fast before the others returned.

"I'm so sorry, guards! But I'm doing this for your safety. If you don't let me take the crystal then the world will fall into danger." Although the guards were groaning in pain, they looked at me with disgusting expressions. They must be thinking two things:

1. I'm completely mad and I've lost my mind.
2. I think that they're stupid and think that they'll fall for my story so that I can continue my robbery with ease.

I sprinted to the base of the statue, where a symbol of the Devil's eye was carved into the surface. Gently, I pressed it, and the panel slid down, revealing a small compartment. A plate slid forward, holding a radiant, red crystal. I'd actually done it! The crystals were real. But there wasn't time to celebrate; I still needed to escape. Just then, Sapphire swooped towards me. I quickly took out the potion, uncapped it, and drank. In a flash, I found myself in the dazzling country of Indonesia.

Chapter 11

Mystics of Indonesia

I opened my eyes and saw myself sitting on a bench. I glanced around but I couldn't find Sapphire. A wave of panic flushed over me. I was glad that at least, I had someone with me on this journey. I bent down and found her stuffy-form under the bench.

Why is she a stuffy now? I gently tucked her in my backpack and started roaming in the city. I found out that I was in Bekasi. Then hunger struck me. So, I went to the park where I first teleported and ate some chips, which were half-eaten by Sapphire. I needed Sapphire right now. She has to tell me about the riddle for the crystal (if there is one).

"Sapphire! Can you become a real bird again?" I whispered, half-hopeful.

"Oh yes! Why not?" she chirped back.

Startled by her sudden voice, I accidentally dropped her onto the ground.

"Ouch! Handle me with care, Enid." she complained, shaking out her feathers as she transformed back.

"Sorry! You always surprise me.", I said, sighing in relief. Then I continued, "Anyway, we're in Bekasi, Indonesia."

"That's great!"

"So, can you give me the next riddle for the second crystal?" I asked. Sapphire nodded.

"The riddle is -FREEDOM FLIES WITH THE WIND, BUT CATCHING IT HAS BEEN MEMORIZED, WITH GOLD ON ITS TIP."

"Wow, Sapphire! Even trickier than the last one." I sighed.

"I know, right?" she replied grinning proudly.

Now, I had to solve it. My mom once taught me a trick: focus on the keywords. The keywords are freedom, Wind, and Gold. I think the gold refers to a monument with a golden peak (tip). It must represent freedom because it says, 'Freedom is memorized.'

I remember, one time, my history teacher gave us some mind-numbing homework about monuments in Indonesia and a few other countries. So, according to my research done for the assignment, the monument must be the 'National Monument', located in Jakarta. It depicts the independence (freedom) of Indonesia. I was in my thoughts when Sapphire screamed in my ear and made me come out of them.

"Enid! Where are you? I mean, you're physically here, but not mentally.", she said, bringing me back to reality.

"Well, I was solving the riddle, which is why I was deep in my thoughts, and you wouldn't help me either, so I gotta do it all by myself." I replied.

"Well, Enid, the riddle exists in this world, and we need you in this world. So, stop escaping to another world."

"I'm not-Forget it. I think I know where the next symbol lies."

Chapter 12

Breeze of Freedom

"Tell me, Enid. Where it lies?", she asked, curious.

"It's in Jakarta."

"Juice?", she exclaimed.

"Oh silly! I said Jakarta, not juice."

"Oops! I heard it wrong. Anyway, what is the symbol?"

"I'll have to check."

I opened Ella's book and spotted a symbol of what looked like wind.

I asked Sapphire, "Do you know which symbol it is?"

"Yes, it's 'Breeze of Freedom'."

"That's it. But there is a problem."

"What is it?", she asked, worriedly.

"The thing is, that this monument is in Jakarta and, we are right now in Bekasi."

"Oh my god! What's with this juice and burger?", she said, annoyed.

"Sapphire! I told you. It's not juice and burger, it's Ja-ka-rta and Be-ka-si. Got it?"

She's so annoying.

"Gotcha.", she replied, again with a grin.

"I think we should just use the potion.", I suggested.

"No! Not a chance.", she exclaimed.

"Why not?"

"You have to use the potion wisely. We have to conserve it for the eight other countries."

"Well, there's 2 bottles of it. Won't it be enough?", I asked.

"Well, one bottle can take us to five countries. The measurements are placed as well. You were lucky you got two. Otherwise, we had to think of another solution for traveling around the world.", she explained.

"Okay! What other ways do you think of traveling?"

"Well, you should know better. I, no longer, understand this world except for chips."

"What do you mean by 'No longer understand the world'?"

"Umm- I mean the world is developing, right? It's changing, isn't it?", she stammered.

"Well. Whatever. We can go by train, then."

"Sounds cool. Wait! How can we travel by rain? We'll have to evaporate?"

"Oh! This bird! I said train, not rain."

"Okey-dokey."

I picked up my backpack and stuffed Sapphire in. Then, went to the nearest metro station. It'll only take thirty minutes to reach Jakarta. That's a relief. As the train arrived, I sat on the seat, nearest to the door and got lost in thoughts- what if I hadn't fought those guards in Cape Town?

Then, we wouldn't have retrieved the crystal and maybe, Ella would've got it before me. But, I'm glad that didn't happen. Only one day before, I was in my school and now here I am, on a world tour adventure to save everyone. Look how the fate changes.

Chapter 13

Heart of Indonesia

Soon, the announcement was made for the next stop, Jakarta. I picked up my backpack and, as the doors opened, I raced out of the train. My jaw dropped when I saw Jakarta's beauty. From my backpack, Sapphire was peeking.

She said, "Well this juice city is worth visiting."

"It's not juice-Forget it. Let's walk to the National Monument."

"Alright."

I walked for a few blocks and reached the destination. But, I wasn't so pleased when I saw where the symbol was. I spotted the symbol on the gold tip while I was all the way here, at the bottom.

"Sapphire! The symbol is way at the top.", I said, with a pale face.

"Okay then! Go grab it.", she said, still intact.

"How can I? I cannot fly, but I do know someone who can.", I said, eyeing her with a grin.

Then, Sapphire made a poker face and transformed into a cat. Unbelievable!

"Element of Land. Now, Enid, I don't have wings anymore. If I don't have wings, then I can't fly. Simple as that."

"Oh! Can't you fly up there and get the crystal for me." I said, pleasingly.

"No. Can't do."

"Ugh! Fine. But, at least tell me the reason."

"Well, I haven't flown this high in centuries."

"In centuries? How old are you?"

"Much, much, much older than you're baby girl.", she smirked.

"I'm not a baby girl. I'm- You know what? I'm not gonna argue with you anymore. You're annoying. Be a bird, a cat, or whatever you want to be. I'll figure something out myself." I said, my voice sharp with frustration.

"That's more like it, Enid." Saying that she stuffed herself in and started to munch chips while I stood there helpless.

I was walking here and there, with my mind out of ideas. I don't think anyone would have an idea of climbing a tower, so high and that too in front of so many people. I was just there, minding my own business, when someone out of the blue, came running towards me and snatched away my cap. I lost my temper.

I shouted, "Hey! Give it back." I sprinted after him. All eyes were on me, but I didn't care. I won't tolerate a thief. We ran for a few blocks and I accidentally stepped on a broken tile, and Woosh! I fell in.

Chapter 14
The Chasm

I lost my balance as the floor crumpled. I started to fall somewhere. I didn't know Indonesia had underground secrets, and it was indeed very deep. I fell on some hay. I was lucky I didn't fall on something rock solid, but wait! What's Hay doing underground? Is there an underground farm?

I picked myself up with a heavy head, trying to regain my balance. It was pitch dark inside. Great, isn't it? This was what I needed.

"Enid! Get me out of here. Where are we now?" Sapphire shouted from my backpack. She must have been swirling in there as I was falling inside.

"Hold on! Wait! I thought I was going to ask you that.", I exclaimed.

"Leave the talk and get me out of this bag." I took her out as well as a torch to lighten up. However, I was thumping with fear.

I said, "Sapphire! Where am I? What's this place? Who created it? Which way should I go? How to get out of here? Why it's so dark? When will you answer? Sapphire!"

"Calm down. So many questions in a row. We'll find a way out.", she said, her voice calm as a breeze.

"How?", I questioned back.

"Somehow.", she replied, grinning.

"Not helping, Sapphire.", I said, as my body trembled.

"Okay! Tell me how you came here. What happened exactly?"

"What happened? Well, a lot. I was there at the monument, pondering over the riddle when suddenly a person came and snatched away my cap. I was furious and ran after him. We ran for a few blocks, and I stepped on a broken tile, and it slid open, pushing me inside this underground thing." I said, in a single breath.

"Okay. Lemme get this straight. You ran for many blocks just for an ordinary cap, and then you didn't even retrieve it and fell into this dark place."

"Practically yes.", I replied with a hint of frustration.

"OMG! A great loss you performed right now.", she teased.

"Not a time for sarcasm Sapphire." I shot back annoyingly. I took a deep breath and continued, "Now that we're stuck in this chasm, we gotta figure out how to get out instead of just being melodramatic."

"You were the one who was being melodramatic a minute ago."

I ignored her taunt and used my torch to see a clear picture. I took a few steps and again stepped on a tile. What's with me and stepping on the wrong tiles today?

"What did you do now?" Sapphire asked in horror.

"I'm sorry. Didn't do it on purpose."

Thank goodness, luck was with me this time. The tile made all the lights in the chasm light up.

"Phew! This time it was for good.", Sapphire said, sighing with relief.

"Sapphire, can I ask you a question?"

"You just did."

"Well, do you know about this place? I feel that it's somehow connected with the quest."

"Lemme think. I'll have to go back to centuries."

After five minutes of thought, she said, "I think my memory's a bit blurry. Why don't you check the book instead? Maybe it'll have some answers."

"Hmm. Good idea." I replied. I opened the book and flipped through the pages until I reached: The Hidden Kingdom of Indania.

Chapter 15
The Hidden Kingdom

I read a few pages from this chapter and discovered that where we're right now, is a hidden and magical kingdom named Indania. It was buried due to Drogeler's evil magic. However, by some genius sorcerers, chasms were made to secure the remaining magic.

I'm pretty sure, that I was brought down due to Sapphire and the book's magic. Now, it's been years since this place was sealed, and judging by its condition, no one entered this chasm until now, when I fell in here while chasing the cap (I'm still upset though, for not catching the cap thief, but anyway.)

I flipped through a few more pages and came across a map. I examined the map and suddenly, it became 3D. It's a magical map. I was witnessing such cool and unbelievable things. But they are a little scary as well. I mean, look at Sapphire. I've got myself a talking bird on this journey or a cat for now. I guess it was a 'Buy 1, Get 1 free' offer.

I studied the map. It hovered in the air, glowing softly. A faint mist swirled around its edges, hiding and revealing secrets. It felt alive, responding to thoughts and intentions, ready to reveal the next step. The castles and villages of the hidden kingdom glimmered, their tiny figures bustling in real time.

After studying it, happiness flushed over me. It wasn't bad that we fell into this chasm because the actual symbol is down here. The symbol up there on the monument was fake.

I exclaimed with excitement bubbling, "Sapphire! I know where the crystal is."

"Uh! Crystal? Weren't you finding a way out first?" She replied, a bit confused.

"Yeah! I was. But I realized that we're at the right place. If we follow the directions from the map, we'll reach the symbol area."

"Bravo!", Sapphire exclaimed.

Chapter 16

Fangs Below

Sapphire and I followed the map carefully, winding through a series of turns before finally arriving at our destination. I was once again close to finding the crystal. Yay!

I said, "Sapphire, according to the map, both the symbol and the crystal should be here."

"Okay.", she replied.

I walked forward and spotted the symbol. I was elated. Then, I started to approach it but Sapphire stopped me. A wave of suspicion flushed over me. Why did she stop me? She didn't want me to grab the crystal?

"What do you think you're doing?" I asked, in a serious tone.

"Why don't you look down?", she replied.

And when I did, my heart nearly stopped. There was a pool of crocodiles, and I misjudged her. When did I start overthinking this much?

"OMG! Thanks a bunch for saving my life.", I sighed with relief.

"Yeah! I just saved you from becoming lunch. Why weren't you looking down?"

"I got excited when I saw the symbol."

"Well, your excitement would've been eaten along with you." she quipped.

"No need of taunting Sapphire. Try to figure out a way to the other side."

I looked around to find something strong enough to take me to the other side. I looked sideways at the area and spotted a sturdy wood log. I summoned all my strength, dragged it to the symbol area, and placed it in between, bridging the gap. Then, I climbed on it and crossed the cavity. I stepped on the floor and pressed the symbol. Suddenly, the whole ground trembled. I spun around as something massive was rising from the pit. A stone crocodile emerged, and its mouth opened wide, from which, came out the red shimmer of the crystal.

"Second crystal captured." I said, triumphant and Sapphire smiled.

"Well, well.", I said with a smirk. "Didn't you say there were crocodiles down there? Turns out they were just mere statues. All of them are harmless."

"Uh?! Don't be so happy just because you got a chance to taunt me.", Sapphire puffed.

"Okay, okay," I replied, grinning. "But honestly, my real reason for celebrating is that we finally found the second crystal."

"It's certainly a time to celebrate, but we still got eight more crystals to find." She replied. "We'll do a huge chips party when we find all of them."

"Yeah! Yeah! You care only about those chips. Let's head to the next destination."

"Where are we heading off next?", asked Sapphire.

"Maldives."

Chapter 17
Deep in the Ocean

Reaching Maldives filled me with joy; it had always been at the top of my travel list. The endless turquoise water and pristine beaches were a dream come true. But my happiness was short-lived.

Sapphire, as expected, had taken her stuffy form again- a cat. Adorable? Absolutely. Annoying? Even more so.

"Sapphire, come on! I need the real you for this." With a blink of shimmer, she transformed.

"Here I am."

This time I barely blinked as I got used to her magical entrances.

I said, "We are in the Maldives, so can you tell me the next riddle?"

"Sure thing. It is- NOT ON GROUND, NOR IN THE AIR, DEEP BENEATH EVERYTHING IS DIFFERENT. LIKE THE CAVES OF THE ANIMALS, BOTH'RE NATURALLY BRILLIANT."

"It's a tough one. Why're they getting tougher by each country?", I whined.

"Don't whine, little Enid. Just use your brain.", she said, teasingly.

"Yeah! Thanks for the advice." I said, taunting her.

"I always give good advice."

She is some bird who takes taunts as compliments.

"Let's break down the riddle," I said.

Caves of animals could mean sea creatures, and deep beneath likely means underwater. My face went pale as it clicked.

"Enid! What's wrong?" Sapphire asked.

"Uh, I might have a huge phobia of water.", I replied, my body shaking at the thought of diving into the water.

She looked stunned.

"Say what! And you're sure we have to go underwater?"

I nodded, swallowing hard.

"Because if it's about deep beneath and brilliance there's only one place that fits, and it's probably underwater.", Sapphire said.

"Well, in conclusion, I've to go underwater and search for the crystal which I can't because of my phobia.", I admitted.

"Then, overcome your phobia. You can do anything you want if your willpower is strong."

"Easier said than done. Once, I went swimming with Ella and I almost drowned. It was traumatic, and I had aqua phobia ever since."

"Did you know swimming back then?"

"Uh? Of course not."

"That's why you drowned. If you learn to swim, then you won't drown."

"Well, I can't learn to swim now, because of the phobia from water."

"Well, how do you drink water then? Don't you feel scared while doing that?"

"Uh?! That's not how phobias work, you birdie."

"Phobia or not, you have to go down there and find the crystal, cuz' if you don't, Ella and Drogeler will win and the world will be at their mercy. You want that?"

"Absolutely not."

"Then, BECOME THE QUEEN OF WATER AND DEFEAT THE PHOBIA OF YOURS.", She declared.

Chapter 18

Queen of Water

Somehow, Sapphire's words encouraged me. I felt motivation suddenly flowing in my veins.

"Alright then. Let's dive in." I said with determination.

"That's the spirit." Exclaimed Sapphire.

We, then headed to the beach. I saw the scuba diving station and went there.

I asked, "Sapphire, can you turn into a fish?"

"Why not?"

I paid the fee and wore my costume. I won't be able to take the book with me. So, before stepping into the boat, I checked for the symbol. It was 'A water wave'. I stepped onto the boat with my heavy costume on and Sapphire stood at the shore, waiting for the chance to transform into a fish.

Then, the boat left the shore, and we were heading to the middle of the sea. My heart raced, sweat trickled, and my face turned white at the thought of jumping into the water. My flashbacks were returning to the time when I almost drowned. Then I recalled Sapphire's words, 'Become the Queen of Water'.

Finally, the time came when we were in the middle of the sea, and we all had to jump. (By we, I mean all the other tourists.) Everybody had already jumped in, and I was the last one left. I gulped.

The boatman said, "What're you waiting for? Go in or I'll push ya."

I heard him and got more terrified. I closed my eyes and leaped in with a huge scream. Seconds later, I was in the water, and I could hear Sapphire's voice.

"Open your eyes, Enid. You gotta see the beauty."

But I just couldn't, and I started to feel as if I was drowning. Sapphire held me with her magic, as my eyes remained closed. I started to calm down and slowly opened my eyes, gasping at the vibrant underwater world.

"OMG! It's breathtaking!", I exclaimed.

"Yes, it is. And you've overcome your phobia. I hereby announce, the new Queen of Water, Enid!"

Chapter 19
Shimmering Depths

I realized my suit was gone, and to my surprise, I could breathe underwater. It felt so natural like I had always known how to do it. It was then that I understood—it had to be Sapphire's magic at work. It felt perfect—almost magical. It was as if the world had opened to me in a new, exciting way.

"Sapphire! Let's go for the search," I called out, eager to explore.

"Aye-Aye, Captain!" came her cheerful reply. Her voice was clear, even beneath the water. I turned to see her, now in her fish form, gracefully swimming beside me.

As we swam together, I couldn't help but notice how stunning Sapphire looked in her fish form. Her scales shimmered in shades of blue and green, catching the light and making her seem like a part of the ocean itself. If there were a competition for the most beautiful fish, she would surely win.

We swam through coral reefs, marvelling at the sight of many fish and other sea animals. A tall structure caught my eye a few meters ahead. As Sapphire and I swam closer, I could hardly believe my eyes. There, beneath the water, was a freakin' underwater library!

It looked like something straight out of a dream. The structure was made of ancient stone, with shelves upon shelves filled with hundreds of books, their spines glowing faintly in the dim, watery light. I had never imagined that something like this could even exist.

I asked, "Sapphire! Did you know about this?"

"Of course not. I stepped into water for the first time.", she replied, her voice full of wonder. I could tell she was just as amazed as I was by the sight of this hidden gem.

We drifted through the aisles, surrounded by the weight of so much knowledge and mystery. The sound of the water was peaceful, almost like a gentle hum, as I took in the sight of books I never thought I'd encounter.

Then, one book caught my attention. Its cover was worn, but still intact, and its title read *The Map of the Underwater City*. That seemed important, I thought. I eagerly flipped through the pages, my curiosity growing with every turn. As I skimmed the map, I noticed a cave marked in a section I hadn't seen before. It was positioned near a cluster of coral, hidden deep within the city's maze-like tunnels.

I paused for a moment, my heart racing. In the movies about mermaids and underwater adventures, caves were always the places where the most valuable treasures or secrets were kept.

They were often the key to a quest or mystery, and this could be exactly what we needed. So, I had this idea maybe the caves will be helpful for me as well (keeping in mind that it's not an action film; it's reality).

I flipped through a few more pages to find what're those caves.

As I read the chapter heading, I knew I had found what we needed. It said: Caves of the Il Regno Degli Animali.

Chapter 20

Mysterious Caves

Sapphire raised an eyebrow and said, "Red? Daily? Chilli? What type of name it is? Is it about some caves that eat red chillis daily?"

"No-no. It is the Caves of the Il regno degli animali." I chuckled.

"OMG! What language are you speaking?"

"Italian."

"That explains the 'Red Daily Chilli.' Anyway, what does it mean?"

"It means: Caves of the Animal Kingdom."

"Then, let's go there and grab the crystal."

Sapphire and I followed the map's directions until we arrived at a vast network of caves. It was enormous, and the map didn't provide many details, so I knew I'd have to navigate this on my own.

"Listen birdie-I mean fishie. If you're magical, then you can sense the crystal. Can't you?"

"Umm-I can try. I don't know if it works in water." She replied.

With that, Sapphire swam toward a few rocks, attempting to sense the crystal. But after a moment, she shook her head and said, "It's not here. Let's go a bit further."

As we moved further, I saw more marine life but no signs of the symbol or the crystal. I was so focused on the surroundings, that I didn't notice I was about to bump into Sapphire.

"Sapphire! What-"

I couldn't say the rest because my jaw dropped. In front of me was a massive cave on which sea animals were carved.

Sapphire said, "I guess we found the right cave."

I said, "So what're we waiting for? Let's go inside."

I was trembling as we entered the pitch-dark cave. Sapphire, equally terrified, pressed close to me, her scaly body shaking. I told myself, "Enid, it's okay. You're gonna be okay. Just stay calm."

But, my reassurance wasn't helping me.

Sapphire noticed me and said, "Enid! You're trembling. If you go any further, your phobia will be back, and it will steal your crown."

"Crown? Oh! That queen of water crown. Wait! You're taunting me while you're also shaking with fear and becoming a fish fry." I smirked.

"Uh?! Fish fry?! How dare you-" She couldn't complete her sentence as in front of us loomed an enormous water creature, glaring at us with unsettling intensity.

He had a pale, wrinkly face and his hair was as pointy as one hundred knives. I could feel shivers passing down my spine.

I thought of tricking it somehow, but that thought soon faded away when I saw the sight of human bones and their SKULLS! I swallowed hard.

What are we gonna do?

Chapter 21

The Water creature

Without thinking twice, I grabbed Sapphire, "Sapphie! Go grab some pebbles."

She gave me a look. "You're forgetting something.", she said, reminding me she had no hands as she's a fish now.

I said, "Oh right! I'll go get em'. You distract the beast."

"What're you going to do with the pebbles, anyway? Paint them?", she said sarcastically.

"If I had paint, maybe. Now go."

Sapphire darted around the creature with incredible speed, her movements swift and unpredictable. I quickly grabbed a handful of pebbles from the cave floor and hurled them at the creature's eyes, ears, and nose. But as I threw them, I realized something odd—he didn't have a nose, reminding me of Voldemort.

I kept up my pebble pelting, aiming for the areas where I hoped he might be most sensitive. At the same time, Sapphire's chaotic distraction was working—she moved in unpredictable patterns, confusing the creature. My plan was simple: we didn't want to hurt him too much, just enough to make him lose his senses, so we could slip past him undetected.

He seemed intimidating, and though I wasn't sure what he could do, I didn't want to risk provoking him too much.

We only needed a little space to get by. With every pebble I threw, the creature let out a low growl of frustration. His movements became more erratic, and then, in pain and irritation, he stomped to the other side of the cave.

He banged his fists against the walls, his large form shaking with anger, but it worked—he had moved far enough away to leave the entrance wide open for us.

"Now's our chance," I whispered, feeling a rush of relief. "Let's get inside and find the crystal."

Sapphire nodded, her fish form shimmering as she swam toward the entrance. I followed close behind her, moving as quietly as I could, hoping not to alert the creature again

Chapter 22

The Water Waves

Sapphire and I giddied up to the cave. From the outside, it seemed dark and horrific but from the inside it's glittering and bright. My eyes were glued to the gemstones on the walls of the cave. It'll cost a fortune, that's for sure. But, I focused on the main goal. We kept moving forward, but the cave seemed to never end.

"Sapphire! When will we reach a point?", I asked, worried.

"How am I supposed to know? It just keeps going."

"Let's not lose hope and keep moving forward. We might reach somewhere."

But it proved me wrong. We came to a DEAD END!

"I can't believe it! The crystal isn't here? Did you sense it right?", I asked.

"Enid! I know this may sound weird, but I'm still able to sense the gemstone. It's here-Magic doesn't lie."

She is right. If magic sensed it, the crystal must be here, just hidden from view. That's when a realization struck me.

"What if? There's something behind this wall?"

"Huh?!" Sapphire replied, puzzled.

I approached the wall and tapped it a few times. It sounded hollow meaning I'm correct. There's something behind it. I was observing it with my hands when suddenly the wall spun around taking me to the other side and leaving Sapphire behind. I was stunned, trying to process what had just happened when I heard Sapphire yelling from the other side

"Oh, Enid! Why do you keep activating traps?", she yelled with frustration.

"It's not a trap. It's where the crystal is."

"The crystal! Good job that you found it."

"I didn't exactly find it."

"What do you mean?"

"Here, all I can see is a pile of boulders on which something is carved."

"Carved?", she repeated. "I'm coming right now. I can't miss this show."

Then, she readied herself to push the wall but instead, the wall pushed her.

"Ouch! This wall is naughty."

"Not naughtier than you are.", I teased.

"Ugh! Wait! Abracadabra!"

Then I heard the wall shaking. The wall collapsed, and its pieces crashed on the floor. My jaw dropped as I witnessed a shark in front of me.

I yelled hysterically. "He- he ate Sapphire. What'll I do now?"

The shark showed no motion, except for its stare. I had no idea whether it blinked or winked at me. Then I heard a voice, casual as could be.

"Enid! Surprised to see me, aye?"

I gasped. "OMG! Why did you scare me like that? You could've told me, so I would've panicked less."

"What did I do?"

"Don't act innocent.", I replied, catching my breath. I continued. "Anyway, since this is carved in some ancient language, you're the only one who can read this."

"Why so confident about that, aye?" she asked.

"Because...you're old." I teased.

"Rude! But I'll try."

She then scanned the text.

"Well, it says that- Ouch!", she yelped.

"What happened? What did I do?"

"You didn't. It did. It says that it'll need a bit of magic to work. It'll show us a magical video.", she replied.

"Woah!"

"Ouch!"

Chapter 23

The Magical Video

A few sparkles of magic drifted away from Sapphire's body which began to form a screen. As it took shape, Sapphire looked visibly drained.

"You okay?" I asked, concerned.

"Yeah! I'm fine. Just a little worn out."

Suddenly, the screen enlarged, flooding the space with binding light. We had to shield our eyes as the brightness grew unbearable. When I opened my eyes again, I found out that we were somewhere else.

"Sapphire! Where are we?"

"We are inside the video."

"What?! That's even possible?"

"Everything's possible with magic, Enidy."

"So... can you create another earth with magic?"

"Um- Exceptions are always there."

I smirked at her. Then, I heard a voice. We looked behind to see human figures, dressed in medieval times, talking.

Then the story began. We should've brought popcorn as Sapphire, and I were going to experience a 3D film.

"I'm Manik Fulhu. Once, I was the most powerful sorcerer in the Maldives. But I chose to share my power to use it for the greater good. Drogeler, another power keeper who had emerged was making the lives of the people miserable. The council of sorcerers was trying to find solutions day and night, however, nothing worked. Everyone else wanted to fight him, thinking that it was the only solution.

But I chose a different path- one rooted in hope and ancient belief. I went for a legend I believed in. The Legend of the Lost Crystal. Once I reached Maldives's ocean, I cast a spell to create gills, allowing me to breathe underwater. As I ventured into the depths, I battled a beast that guarded the caves. Pushing forward, I kept moving through endless tunnels, hoping to reach the crystal. Finally, I found what seemed to be the victory-but it was only a dead end. My heart sank.

No crystal, no hope.

With hope lost, I turned back. I guess it was fate. I thought to do the same as everybody else-Fight the beast and become its feast. But just as I began my return, the monster reappeared, now with an army at its side, ready to finish me off. In those final moments, I understood the gravity of my situation.

I left a message for anyone who might find it, a warning, a plea for understanding.

Then, with the remains of my magic, I erased all the memories of magic from humanity, hoping to protect them from the darkness that had come.

As I faced the end, the last thing I saw was a ruby-coloured laser cutting through the cave wall.

Chapter 24
The Lost Awakened

Sapphire and I were stunned by Manik Fulhu's speech. I couldn't help but wonder why he hadn't found the crystal, even after reaching the point where we now stand.

"Wait a minute!" Sapphire exclaimed. "His last name is Fulhu, right? I can't remember this term. Well, I'm 2,023 years old. Of course, my memory's a bit blurry!"

"Woah! You're that old! Still no sense of wisdom and advice."

"Cut the sarcasm, will ya? Wait! I think I remember now!"

"What do you remember?"

"Fulhu was Ronia's best and favourite cousin.", Sapphire said. "He's lying right now. All of his ancestors practised dark magic."

I gasped. "You can't be serious."

"I am dead serious. Manik is Fulhu's last descendant. The magical video he created has a dark purpose. We must leave."

Before I could respond, a heavy voice echoed around us.

"BE WISE AND LEAVE."

"Just trying to scare us.", I muttered.

"We need to find the crystal. It's not safe to swim back; we can use the potion to escape.", Sapphire suggested.

As the video ended, I moved forward to the carved boulders scanning for the water wave symbol. I spotted it and pressed it, leading a plate forward on which the gemstone stood firmly. I grabbed it and started to search for the potion only to realize that I had left my bag on the shore.

"Sapphie! I left my backpack on the beach. How are we going to go back?"

"Well, there's no choice but to swim."

"What if the monster comes back again like he did at the time of Manik Fulhu."

"Well, we destroyed his senses. He can't even call an army now."

"But, what if-"

"No what ifs. Let's move."

We flipped the wall which took us back to the cave's pathway. We then swam faster than the speed of light, with adrenaline pumping. Just as we reached the opening, I felt someone's hand brush against mine. I gasped and froze, glancing back, but no one was there.

Sapphire asked, "Whatcha stopped for?"

"I just felt someone touch my hand. It's probably a seaweed or something."

"Oh. Okay. Then let's move forward."

As we turned our heads, a scream escaped us, raw and filled with terror. Manik Fulhu stood before us, his lips twisted into a cruel grin. My heart pounded in my chest, each beat louder than the last, as if the water had grown heavier with his presence. The world seemed to freeze, every muscle in our bodies was screaming to move, but we were paralyzed by his presence. Even though Sapphire and I tried to swim around him, he blocked our path with a quick, unsettling movement.

"Finally," he sneered, "Someone comes for the gemstone with a talking fish. How interesting."

"How... how are you still alive?", these were the only words that escaped my mouth.

"Alive?" His grin widened. "No, not alive. A spirit."

His words sent a chill through us. We trembled, knowing there was no escape.

"Now, now. Hand over the crystal, and I'll let you leave." His voice was cold, dripping with menace. I was too shocked to reply, but I couldn't give him the crystal.

"NO!" I blurted.

His eyes darkened. "What did you say?"

"I said NO! You won't get the crystal, foolu." I twisted his name to provoke him. His smirk vanished.

"You shouldn't have said that. Especially twisting my name."

"Oh, what are you gonna do? Use your foolu powers on me?"

His glare sharpened, and my boldness vanished. I had pushed him too far. After all, he was a powerful sorcerer.

"You won't lay hands on the crystal.", Sapphire said, her voice steady. She gave me a quick signal to swim past him, her eyes telling me she would handle it.

"I'm not leaving you alone," I whispered.

"Trust me."

Reluctantly, I swam past, heart racing, as Manik Fulhu moved to follow. But before he could, Sapphire struck, her powers surging toward him. I didn't look back. Minutes later, she emerged from the cave, and we swam to the shore in silence. I didn't ask what she did to him because honestly, I didn't want to know. Whatever it was, it worked.

As we reached the shore, I noticed a crowd gathered near the diving station, along with a rescue boat. Why were they here? Then it hit me-they must be searching for me. I had been underwater for so long.

Of course, they had no idea that a girl with aqua phobia had swum beneath the waves, guided by a magical fish, in search of a red magical crystal.

They wouldn't know about the noseless creature we fought or the spirit of a 1000-year-old (or more) sorcerer we barely escaped. And if I told someone what happened, who would believe me? I can hardly believe it myself!

I emerged from the water, dripping and exhausted, and quickly grabbed my backpack despite my fatigue.

Just then, I heard a policeman shout, "There she is!"

I didn't want to answer any of their questions. They would first scold me, then ask me how I survived, and then ask why I was down there for so long. If I tell them the reasons, then I'll be meat. They'll call my mother stating that I'm not stable and have to see a doctor.

So, I bolted. Running as fast as I could, I weaved through the crowd until I reached a quiet spot, far from the police. Without a second thought, I pulled out the potion and drank it. In the blink of an eye, I found myself standing in the vibrant, sunlit streets of Spain, where music filled the air and people danced around me.

Chapter 25

Under the Spanish Sky

How would you feel walking through a lively street, where dancers perform Flamenco, musicians play enchanting melodies, and everyone radiates warmth and appreciation?

I can tell you how I feel-I'm elated! Spain is magnificent. I've always dreamed of visiting, longing to join the street dancers in their Flamenco routines, the only dance I truly know. The energy here is contagious, and I can't help but smile as I soak it all in.

"Enid! Have you admired all the beauty or some is left, because time is running fast as Ella is on the loose." Sapphire said, pulling me back to reality.

"Oh right! I got distracted."

As I glanced around, I noticed several people staring at me, likely wondering why I was talking to myself or someone invisible. Those who hadn't seen my conversation with Sapphire must have heard her mention 'Ella on the loose' and were probably imagining some dangerous prisoner was on the run. Oops! What to do with this bird?

I found an isolated spot and sat down to read the book, I mean, the grimoire. I checked the symbol, and it's a star in the dark.

I asked, "Well, what's the riddle this time?"

"IT SHINES ALONE IN THE DARK, WITHOUT ANY REST; EVERYONE LIVES ON ITS SPARK."

"Okay. Doesn't look so hard.", I said.

I picked up the key words-Shines alone, Dark and Spark.

"Sapphie, you say that the symbol is always on some monument, aye?"

"Not true. It can be on a mountain, on a building, or even on a public toilet." She replied, grinning.

"What? Are you serious? On a public toilet! Hold your tongue."

"I don't have a tongue, I've a beak. I can use that to peck you."

"No, thank you. I would rather focus on the riddle."

'It shines alone' refers to the star symbol but what does it mean by, 'without any rest and everybody lives on its spark'? Even if a star twinkles, it's not needed by any of us to live. I mean, it's not essential (like the sun) and we can say that it takes a rest when the sun comes up.

"Sapphire! I've figured the first part of the riddle but the second, not so much. Why don't we roam around the city? Maybe we'll find an answer there."

"If you say so.", she replied.

That was an excuse to wander around the city. It's my dream place after all. So, it won't take much time and maybe

I'll get an idea to solve the second part of the riddle. So, it was a partial excuse. We set off to explore the city, in the heart of Spain, Madrid. It was so breathtaking. I had some cash with me, so I savoured the street food. There, again, I spotted a group of dancers on the street. I stood there to watch their show. Their coordination was spectacular, and I couldn't help but smile.

Suddenly, one of the girls approached me, "Senorita! I very much like your dance. Please join us. It would make us happy."

As she spoke, I realized I had unconsciously started dancing along with them. I could never pass up a chance to embarrass myself, could I? She pulled me, and we all danced together as the crowd cheered on. I felt the rush of adrenaline go higher as I danced and twirled. Then, Sapphire came flying and sat on my head, striking her beak.

I distanced myself from the girls and asked Sapphie, "What happened?"

"What happened!? You got distracted again! Remember why you're here?"

"I didn't get distracted, I got an opportunity to practice my dancing skills because in school if I even start dancing, I'll first have to face the bullies.", I protested.

"You can grab any opportunity later but please focus on the objective. The objective of being here.", she replied.

"I know. I know. I've been at it for two days straight. Haven't even got a peace of mind." I replied in frustration.

"Enid! I know it's been difficult for you to grasp the truth of your friend's betrayal and the need to embark on this journey to save the world. Although you should've been enjoying your teenage life, you still chose to come along and find the crystal. That takes a lot of courage, and I appreciate that.", she said calmly.

I cooled down. She's right. I've to focus on the crystals. Sapphire was about to say some more when the dancing lady grabbed my hand and started to drag me.

"Excuse me? Where are you taking me?", I asked confused.

"Hermosa Senorita (Beautiful Miss), please come along and dress up like us and we shall dance togetherrr.", she replied.

She emphasized 'together'. But I can't go and waste my time on dancing. I've spent enough time in the city. I've to go and search for the crystal.

So, I said, "Sorry Dancing lady. But I won't be able to dance with you guys. I gotta go somewhere."

"Oh! Triste! (sad). Please join us, senorita.", she said dramatically.

She didn't listen to me and still dragged me even when I neglected it. She took me to her dressing van and every lady there greeted me kindly. The people here are very nice.

"Hola, senorita."

"Hola" I replied with a grin.

Then, one of the ladies took me and kinda shoved me to a corner, where many robotic hands were attached. I guess, that was a dressing robot.

She said, "Vertirse (Dress up). We're waiting for you."

Then, she closed the curtain, and the machine did my hair and makeup while I dressed up in a dazzling flamenco dress.

Chapter 26

Echoes of Flamenco

I stepped out of the dressing room and every lady gasped. When I looked in the mirror, I realized that the robot had done an impressive job. The dress I'm wearing is a striking shade of deep red, its fabric rich and flowing like molten lava. It is both bold and graceful, a perfect balance of strength and beauty.

One of them said, "This dress suits you very well, Senorita. Let's go out and dance."

Then they took my hand and led me outside. I was so overjoyed that I even forgot about my backpack in which the crystals were kept. I started dancing with everyone else, and the crowd erupted with applause.

While dancing, I suddenly remembered that my bag was in the cabin, but I didn't worry much because these ladies were nice, and no one could steal. Besides, the van was locked. I danced my heart out till it was evening. I didn't even realize how much time went by. We, girls, stopped and went towards the cabin.

"You first go and change, Senorita." Alya said, the group's leader.

"Okay, Gracias." I spoke.

I went inside and changed. Today was pure joy. The rhythm of the guitar and the claps of the castanets filled the air. I laughed with my new friends, sharing steps. Every movement felt light, every beat a celebration.

I stepped out of the dressing room but couldn't find any of the girls there. Then I spotted; my backpack wasn't there. A wave of panic surged over me.

"Alya! Camila! Carmen! Where are you all?" I shouted but no one answered.

I again called out their names, but nobody came. Rushing to the door, I tried to turn the handle, but it was locked from the outside. Those girls fooled me. They stole my valuables and locked me inside.

Why was I this blind to trust them? Why I didn't listen to Sapphire? I sat down, leaning against the door, sad and grieved. But I couldn't sit back and whine. I have to do something. I looked around and saw a few bobby pins lying on the dresser. I got up, picked up the pin, and tried unlocking the door. Luckily, I succeeded. Yes!

I barged the door open, descended the stairs, and saw a man at a distance. So, I approached him and asked, "Um- Hello. Did you see a group of flamenco dancers leaving this cabin?" I hope he knows English.

"Yes. I did. They headed that way."

The man pointed into a dark alleyway. I thanked the guy and dashed to the alleyway. I don't know whether they're on Ella's side or they're usual robbers, I'm going to make them regret stealing from me.

Chapter 27

Sapphire's POV

I peeked from the backpack, and we were somewhere else. It seemed like a dressing room, but Enid wasn't there. It must be the dressing cabin of the dancing girls who were dragging Enid. Now, I'll have to wait for her because I can't even get out.

After so many hours, I heard the girls' voices. I was about to get out when I heard Spanish. It wasn't Enid who was talking. They were the Flamenco girls. What's happening? Then, one of them told Enid to change. Enid went into the changing room. Then, I saw one of them approaching the backpack, I quickly hid and made myself look lifeless. I realized that the girl was picking the bag up and leaving the cabin. I knew these dancing ladies were up to no good. I had to alert Enid, so an idea struck me.

Only this girl who picked up the backpack is stepping out, so I'll just lock up the rest. That way, Enid might confront them as she'll see the backpack gone and the rest of the girls stuck inside. Great idea. I'm a genius!

I carried out my plan with pleasure until I realized I had made a huge mistake. I peeked from the backpack in a way that no one would spot me and gasped. Instead of trapping the dancing thieves, I locked up Enid. Panic surged over me. What now? How can I be such a klutz?

I thought hard like Enid does every time I give her riddles. Then, an idea sparked; hopefully better than my last one. I'd leave a magical trail for Enid to follow.

Using my magic, I wrote (Only you can see this) Enid, you better follow this trail. Make sure you teach these thieves a lesson. From Sapphire.

I hope she breaks out of the cabin and reaches me as soon as possible, by following the trail.

Chapter 28

Back to Enid's POV

As I entered the alleyway, my spine shook due to fear. It's not like I've got a phobia of darkness, but it can be scary at times. Why did these robbers have to go there? As they took my backpack with them, I didn't even have my flashlight. But no matter how many phobias I've, I'll still rise and bring my inner bravery to life.

I walked a few meters straight until I reached a diversion. How can I choose now? I looked around for a signboard, knowing that there wouldn't be such a thing in this alley.

Suddenly, something lit up. I looked at the floor and realized it was a magical trail from Sapphire. That little bird! She's amazing! Thanks to this, I feel less afraid now and I'll also reach the thieves' lair in no time.

I followed the magical trail until I reached a house, the only house with the lights on. I peeked through the window and spotted the thieves. Besides Alya, my backpack was on the table and all the crystals were taken out. They're going to sell those to earn a fortune. I can't let that happen. How can I retrieve the crystals from them? A disguise? A diversion? No! I'll face them as I am.

They need to know who I am and with whom they messed with. The real show starts when they open the door.

I knocked. Camila came to the door, and the moment she opened it, I swung at her perfect, fake nose. She stumbled back, landing with a soft thud on the floor. All the girls were alerted and started to sweat in fear.

I said, "Hey robbers! Do you know whom you stole from? Somebody who has fought the guards at a public place, crossed a crocodile lake and fought a ferocious, noseless monster at the bottom of the Indian Ocean. You don't want to mess with me."

"What nonsense are you speeaking, Eenid?" Alya said.

"You're gonna get this 'nonsense' once you're on the floor with broken legs.", I exclaimed with air quotes.

"Girls! Stop her." Alya commanded her minions.

But I wasn't scared. Good thing I knew martial arts. I fought with everything I had, bringing them down one by one. I managed to knock them off their feet. They all lay on the floor, dazed, while Alya stood frozen in the corner, eyes wide with fear.

"Take your bag and jewels," she said, her voice shaky, "and leave us alone."

"Good thing you realized.", I said, feeling victorious.

Chapter 29

Payback

I grabbed the crystals, stuffed them into my backpack, and left their house. I ran for a few meters until I reached a fountain and sat on the edge, breathless. Reaching into my backpack, I gently pulled out Sapphire. She looked up at me with teary eyes.

"Oh, Enid! I thought I'd lost you. I thought that we'd never see each other again," she said dramatically.

Then, she turned into a cat to scare me. Mischievous cat, bird, fish or let's just say magical creature.

"I'm sorry. I should've listened to you.", I said.

"Yeah! You should be. Even after I locked you up, I didn't lose hope." She grinned mischievously and said, "Wait, I shouldn't have said that."

"You did what!?" I exclaimed. "It's good that I had a bobby pin with me, otherwise I wouldn't have got out while you would been the thieves' keychain." I exclaimed.

"Saucy pin? Sounds tasty. You should've brought some for me."

"Not saucy pin, it's bobby pin. Ugh, never mind. I'm just glad we've reunited."

"Aww! You're making me cry.", she said, playfully.

"Haha."

We both laughed and then fell into a comfortable silence, resting by the fountain for a few minutes. After a few minutes, I broke the silence and said, "We should start searching for the crystal. We've lost a lot of time due to my carelessness."

"It's okay. Don't worry. The good thing is that you've learned the lesson. You have, right?"

"Yup. Lesson learned. Now, let's solve the second part of the riddle and move on to the next country."

"Si, Enid (Yes Enid)."

Chapter 30

Fountain of Life

"What moves without rest? Can you figure it out? I asked.

"Nope. The riddle's tough.", she replied.

"If we can't figure out the riddle then we won't be able to find the place where the crystal is located.", I said.

I tried to think hard but nothing came up in my mind; It was blank. I leaned back on the support of the fountain wall. The water flowing gave a cool environment, which was needed due to the Crystal Marathon.

That's when I noticed that running water never rests. Can that be it? But how it's connected to the star symbol?

I stood up and observed the fountain.

"Watcha doin' there?" asked Sapphire.

"Nothing. Just observing the fountain.", I replied.

"Why? You dropped your brain in there?", she taunted.

"Nope! Yours is in there. Just finding that." I rolled my eyes in sarcasm and continued my observation.

On the wall of the fountain's base was something carved. The Star Symbol! My mouth opened wide when I spotted it.

I jumped in excitement and said, "Sapphie. Look what I found."

"You found your brain?"

"No, daft bird! The symbol. It's here."

"Really?"

I looked closely and yes-It was the symbol. I couldn't have chosen a better resting place than this.

"How it is connected to the riddle?", Sapphire asked, curious.

"Well, 'shines alone' refers to the stars in the night sky, and 'without rest' refers to the running water of the fountain on which the symbol is carved."

"Ooo. Groovy.", she replied.

I chuckled. I moved forward, pressed the symbol gently, and waited for something to happen. But nothing did. Why? The symbol is right here or what if it's fake like it was in Indonesia? But this answer fits the riddle. Then, what's the problem? What was I missing?

"Are you sure you solved the riddle right?" Sapphire asked, doubtful.

"I'm a hundred percent sure."

I pondered over it again and came up with a theory.

"What if, the symbol has to shine somehow?"

"What do you mean?"

"I mean, it says to shine alone in the dark. Maybe the symbol will shine when it's dusk. When the moonlight will fall on it."

"Woah! That's possible. Hope it works."

Chapter 31
Under the Moonlight

"I hope so too." I checked my phone and searched when it would be dusk in Madrid. It'll be at 10:01 PM.

"We'll have to wait for half an hour.", I informed Sapphire.

"Oh no! This long?", Sapphire exclaimed.

"Yes! Unfortunately, yes." I sighed. "But, it's worth waiting for."

"As we've to wait, why don't you get me some chips?" she said, grinning.

"Fine, you little hungry creature." I chuckled.

AFTER HALF AN HOUR

I checked my phone for the time, and it was nearly dusk. Sapphire and I positioned ourselves, waiting for the moonlight to fall upon the star symbol. Today, was a full moon night. Thank goodness the moon was on our side. I glanced sideways to see whether there were any people.

There were a few, but far away from us so that won't be a problem.

I turned back to see the symbol glowing as moonlight was falling on it. It's freaking working. I was right!

I said, "Sapphie! It's working."

Sapphire was overjoyed. After a few minutes, the moonlight completely covered the symbol, and it was shimmering, and it was so... magical. Suddenly, the symbol's brightness grew so high, that Sapphire and I had to close our eyes. When I opened them again, I saw that I had entered a magical place just like I did in the Maldives.

In front of me, was the enormous star symbol with the crystal inside it. My surroundings seemed alive but I couldn't admire it all. So, I grabbed the crystal and returned to the fountain.

Chapter 32
Serenity of Greece

I kept the fourth gemstone in my bag, took out the potion, drank it, and teleported to the fifth country, Greece. I opened my eyes to see that I landed in an alleyway. Now, I hate alleys! I ran back to the main road (or street) and sunlight hit my eyes, so it took time to adjust.

When my eyes adjusted, they flew wide open upon seeing the beautiful infrastructure of Santorini, Greece. But Enid! Don't get distracted this time. Stay focused.

"I hope some boatman, or food stall person, or any stranger doesn't fool you this time.", Sapphire said, sarcastically.

"No, they won't. Even if something like the Spain episode happens, they'll get the same fate as Alya and her team.", I replied, proudly.

"You're saying that so proudly! BOASTFUL ENID!"

I ignored her taunts and found a place to check the next symbol. I flipped through the pages and the symbol was- A Dragon. I gulped. What relation does Greece have with dragons? Magic is crazy.

"Sapphie! What's the riddle?" I asked.

I was sure it was going to be a hundred times harder than the last ones.

Sapphire answered, "IT GIVES IT IN THE HANDS OF THE LOYAL, BUT SLAYS THE VILLAINOUS WITH FOIL. EITHER KILL IT OR MAKE IT SMILE, IF YOU FAIL TO CHOOSE, YOU'LL BE IN THE GRAVE IN A WHILE."

But it was a thousand times more terrifying than the last ones.

"Are you sure that's the riddle?", I asked, quivering with terror.

"Yup. Why you ask? Because of the last line?"

"Not only the last line, but the entire riddle!", I exclaimed.

Sapphire laughed at my statement. She replied, "At least the riddle is not as scary as Manik Fulhu's ghost."

"Of course it is."

Sapphire giggled and I focused on solving the creepy riddle. I suppose the keywords are Hands of loyal, villainous, smile, and graves. My nerves are shaking upon saying the riddle. If the riddle is this scary, then what'll the way to finding the crystal be like? Can't even imagine.

I said, "Sapphire, what if 'hands of loyal' means the hands of the person who deserves the crystal?"

"Hmm. Makes sense.", after a thought, she continued, "If 'loyal' means the deserving then 'villainous' refers to the one who wants the crystal for the wrong means."

"Yes! Like Ella and Drogeler." I exclaimed.

"But the second part of this riddle is deadly.", Sapphire spoke.

Sapphire and I were solving the riddle, part by part when the crowd broke into chaos, people screaming and shouting in fear. Faces were pale, and eyes were wide with panic. Everyone pushed and shoved, trying to get away. The noise was deafening—cries, hurried footsteps, and desperate voices filled the air. Fear spread like wildfire as people ran. Children were crying, belongings were abandoned, and the ground shook with the pounding of fleeing footsteps.

When I looked around, everything seemed normal—nothing to panic about. But when I looked up at the sky, my heart stopped. What I saw was terrifying beyond words. A chill ran through me, and fear took over as I stood frozen, unable to believe what I saw.

Chapter 33

The Scarlet Beast

The sky over Greece darkened as if the sun had been swallowed. A strange, metallic scent filled the air, thick and suffocating and a deafening roar shook the air. A massive, blood-red dragon with needle-sharp teeth and glaring yellow eyes was floating above Greece.

Wasn't I the one who asked what's the relation of Greece with dragons? Well, the dragon itself has come to answer my question. Personally. I turned to Sapphire, but she looked horrible. She was turning red in fear.

I asked, "Sapphire what's happening to you?"

"I'm a-a-allergic to dragons."

"What?" I exasperated.

"When the dragon's scales hit a person's skin, he/she becomes allergic to them. Years ago, I was hit by a dragon while fighting against him.", she explained.

"If you're allergic to dragons, then what'll I do?", I gasped.

"Don't worry. I'll go and find something to help."

"Find something? What'll I do till then?"

"You've two choices- If you're scared so go and hide, but if you're bold and eager to save everyone, then confront the villain.", Sapphire spoke calmly.

Saying that she vanished into thin air while the windows shattered miles away, and birds plummeted from the sky, their wings frozen mid-flap due to the dragon's fury. I stood there, with sweat dripping off my face.

Chapter 34
Sapphire's POV (Part 2)

I was already terrified to tell the riddle, but the moment I saw the massive dragon in the sky, my heart stopped. My soul practically left my body as I stared at the enormous creature. Its blood-red scales gleamed like molten fire, and its yellow eyes pierced through me like daggers. I could hardly believe my eyes. To make matters worse, I'm allergic to dragons.

But the good part is that I know how to defeat them. The real question is—how will Enid face this beast alone while I'm away trying to find the solution?

I glanced at her. She was frozen in fear, her eyes wide as she watched the dragon circle overhead. But even through her fear, I saw strength. Enid had come so far, battling her way through so many challenges. She's stronger than she knows. I believe in her.

So, I told her that I was leaving to find help for her. Her fear shifted into confusion, but there was no time to explain. I hated the thought of leaving her in this dangerous situation, but staying here without a plan would only make things worse.

I teleported to a place—a field filled with Red Kalanchoe flowers.

These flowers symbolize endurance and calm, thriving in even the harshest conditions, which is why they have a calming effect on dragons. If I could gather enough, it might just give us a chance to stop the dragon from creating havoc. Without wasting a second, I plucked a large bunch of the vibrant flowers and teleported back to where I had left Enid.

I returned but my heart shattered into pieces. The once-quiet place was now in ruins. The ground was scorched, buildings lay in rubble, and smoke filled the air. Enid was on the ground, injured. Her breathing was laboured, and her clothes were torn, but when I looked into her eyes, I saw something incredible- determination.

She was hurt, but she hadn't given up. The fire in her gaze told me that she was ready to fight, no matter the odds. My guilt for leaving her faded slightly. I knew I had done the right thing by coming back with a plan. Now, together, we had a chance. A chance to win against this dreadful creature.

Chapter 35

Determination

Sapphire disappeared leaving me behind and fear appeared inside me. I was all alone with no idea how to calm down this dragon.

I don't even have magic, how am I supposed to handle it while it keeps demolishing the place? People were running all around in panic and screams shook the place.

People were shouting, "Drakon! Drakon! (Dragon!) Treximo! Treximo! (Run!)"

I had no idea what this meant, nor did I have the time to google translate this. Moreover, when the beast emitted fire in the sky, the screams of people increased, and I know it must've been beyond 120 decibels.

People were crying hard, and some tall buildings caught fire. I was sweating and felt a bit of dizziness. Then, I saw the dragon approaching a few people who were stuck under a tree and were shouting harshly for help. It glared at them and released heavy smoke through his nostrils. I couldn't let the dragon hurt those innocent people.

Suddenly, I felt rage and wrath build up inside me, as I thought of the people getting hurt by the dragon. I won't let that happen.

As the dragon opened his mouth to blow fire, I picked up a dustbin, and with all force, threw it in his mouth, with my heart pounding. The dustbin landed in its mouth and to my surprise, he started munching the dustbin.

Maybe, he quite enjoys eating dustbins. Another idea struck me. I can stop the dragon from rampaging by throwing things in his mouth, till Sapphire comes back. Before that plan, I ran to the people who were stuck and assisted them in getting out.

"Efcharisto! (Thank you)", they said with happy tears and relief.

When I looked up, I saw the dragon glaring at me and I could read his expressions. His expression probably said, "I'll eat you."

Suddenly, my boldness vanished.

I said, "You see, dragon. I'm a just normal girl who was trying to live a normal teenage life, however, I got dragged into this crystal chase and 'saving the world' chase. So, don't try to make me meat and we'll talk. Alright?"

It didn't answer and just glared at me. I had no idea what it was going to do next. I thought maybe it listened to my words and understood, but they weren't that persuasive.

And that's the reason it roared and emitted fire in the sky. That's when I knew that it was my cue to leave.

I ran in the other direction for my life. While running, I looked back and saw that it was coming after me. My plan of throwing things to keep him distracted backfired. Instead, I had to run a marathon as my life was at stake. Wait! What was that in its mouth? Was it- No time to think! It's still after me.

I kept running till I was out of breath, while the dragon was full of energy, coming after me with full force. Still, I ran. I came to a point where my legs gave up, and I couldn't breathe. I turned around to face the dragon. It glared at me and its smoke caused me to cough. Suddenly, it used its tail and hit me hard, making me fall on the other side. Luckily, I didn't get much injury, but I was lying on the ground, exhausted and wounded.

I saw the dragon leave me and go to other people. I can't let it hurt others. Despite my wounds and bruises, I stood up and shouted, "Don't you dare hurt others! If you will, you'll have to face me."

The dragon smirked at my statement.

"Pretty brave, you are, for your age." She spoke.

I was astonished by the revelation that it could talk and that it was a 'she'. However, I was not going to step back.

I said, flushing with confidence, "Yes. I am, and I'll not let you hurt others. What benefit are you getting from devastating the place?"

She burst into laughter at my question and then suddenly stopped, fixing me with an outraged look.

Her unblinking amber eyes fixed their gaze on me while I glistened with sweat, and my hands trembled in response. She knew she had the upper hand.

Suddenly, she puffed up and began emitting fire. Startled, I quickly moved out of the way, narrowly avoiding being burned by the flames. I fell to the ground, my body aching intensely.

I somehow got up, and I could feel tears slipping from my eyes due to the helplessness.

Chapter 36
The Saviour Flowers

The dragon smirked as she saw me wounded, exhausted, and helpless. Then I heard a scream, "I'm coming, Enid! Don't lose hope."

I turned to look, and it was Sapphire. She was back, and she had a bunch of red flowers in her hands. I didn't know what it was for, but I'm glad she returned, just on time, before I got baked.

"You've got a bird as your saviour. How hilarious!", the dragon said sarcastically.

"No! I've got the Red Kalanchoe as the saviour." Saying that Sapphire powdered the flowers and threw the mixture all over the dragon. The dragon's wild and chaotic behaviour was instantly quelled by the dispersing red kalanchoe powder.

It's amazing how quickly things can change! Now, the once ferocious dragon is as calm as a breeze, purring like a cat. I cautiously approached her, gently patting her head, relieved that she had been calmed down. She didn't refuse and just let me.

People around sighed with relief at the sight but were still terrified so they stayed low.

I said, "Good girl!"

I saw Sapphire in a corner and suddenly remembered something.

I excused myself from the dragon and said, "Sapphire! You know what I saw while fighting the dragon?"

"What? Her yellow teeth?", she asked.

"No silly! I saw a bright ruby light coming out of her mouth."

"What!?", she gasped.

"Yes! I think I know the answer to the riddle. The fifth crystal is actually in her mouth."

"I get it now. We had to calm her down and that way we could take the gemstone. Only the one with a kind heart can calm her down.", Sapphire explained.

"Exactly."

Sapphire and I went back to the dragon.

I asked, "What's your name?"

"Hera. I'm the vasilissa (queen) of the Drakon Kingdom."

"Woah! That's so cool. Well, Queen Hera, can you help us?"

"How can I serve you?"

"There's a precious stone present in your mouth. The world needs it."

"How'll I know you'll use it for the good?", Hera questioned.

"Read my heart."

Hera was astonished at my statement.

I continued, "I've read in my book, I mean, Grimoire, that dragons can read the hearts of humans. Please do so."

The dragon agreed and started chanting some spells. After a few seconds, she smiled and said, "I see. You are worthy. Find the other crystals as well and save the world from evil. Don't let that monster, Drogeler win."

"I'll not let that happen. Drogeler will not get his hands on the crystal.", I exclaimed.

"Also include your schoolmate. I read her betrayal. I'm sorry."

"It's okay. I've just agreed with the reality that she had to turn out like this.", I said with a depressed sigh.

She smiled and then opened her huge mouth wide open, and I forwarded my hand to grab the crystal. Just when, I got my hands on it, a sword out of nowhere appeared and sliced through Hera's neck.

I was abruptly shoved aside, catching me off guard. In the chaos, a hand swiftly snatched the crystal. Anger and shock surged through me as I tried to process what had just happened. Before I could react, another forceful push sent me sprawling to the ground with a resounding thud. Fury boiled over as I scrambled to my feet, determined to confront the culprit.

My eyes locked onto the one face I had desperately hoped to avoid—the very person I dreaded seeing most.

Chapter 37

End of the Beginning

"What did you just do, you traitor?" I asked, with my rage and fury unexplainable.

"Can't you see? I slayed it." Ella answered.

"Why are you here?", I asked furiously.

"To take what's mine.", she replied with a smirk.

"Yours? The Crystal? In your dreams, traitor.", I shouted.

"You got no powers. You're just a little weakling."

That was the last straw. I couldn't even control my expressions of anger and vexation. But, deep down these expressions hid the feelings of hurt and betrayal. But, I won't let them take the best of me.

"You know? I had a friend once, who gave me courage and confidence when I needed it. Unfortunately, she left her family, friends, and home just to become a mere puppet of a powerless creature who's yearning to be set free and grab the crystals to attain back his abilities. Can't believe he's this helpless that he's taking help from its enemy's gemstones." I shouted at her, with my blood boiling.

I could see Ella annoyed at my statement. She said, "You'll regret saying that."

With that, she swung her sword shooting laser beams at me. Even if she had a magical sword, she still couldn't beat my intelligence. I started to sprint, in my defence, barely saving myself from her shots. I kept running but she was quick. I was running out of breath, but I still had to go otherwise, I would be meat. Suddenly, I stepped on something and slipped.

"Gave up so easily?" she smirked.

She pointed her sword at me, and I just closed my eyes. When I opened them, I realized nothing had happened to me. That's because a dragon protected me. But wait a minute! Hera's dead. Then, who's this?

"Run, Enid! Take the crystals and run as far as you can. Keep them safe with you." said Sapphire.

It was Sapphire, who transformed into a dragon to shield me. Smart, she is! I picked myself up and ran in the other direction for my life. I could hear the clashes between Ella and Sapphire but there was nothing I could do except for keeping the crystals safe, so I ran away. Buildings were shattered and parts of their roofs were falling. I narrowly escaped them. What a horrible loss of property!

After a huge marathon, I looked back and saw that I was distant from the battle, so I stopped there to recharge my energy. The battle of the two was intense. Ella charged, her sword flashing as she faced Sapphire in her dragon form.

She roared, flames bursting from its jaws and scorching the ground where Ella had just stood. She leaped back, landing with ease, her eyes burning with irritation and rage. With a quick motion, her sword started shooting bright laser beams. Sapphire, in her defence, emitted a huge amount of fire and Ella barely escaped it. They kept clashing with each other but none stopped.

I was observing the two when I noticed a solar panel, from one of the buildings falling. A laser beam hit the polished surface of the panel and it reflected. An idea hit me like a lightning bolt. What if, I collect a lot of solar panels and arrange them in a way so that the beam hits it and gets reflected? That way Ella's laser beams will backfire on her.

Brilliant!

The only problem is that there aren't many solar panels, or any other reflecting surface needed to execute the plan. I looked around and saw a truck on which it was written something in Greek, but I recognized the truck as a mirror transporting truck from its mirror illustration. I ran to the man, who was getting down from his seat.

I asked, "Sir, would you mind if I borrowed your truck?"

He didn't understand me and said, "I no English. Trexe gia ti zo sou (Run for your life)."

I guess he means yes. I climbed into the driving seat. The engine roared as I pushed the accelerator to its limit, the truck surging forward at high speed. I was driving like a maniac, and people were legit screaming at me.

"Sorry guys! But I'm doing this for your safety. Otherwise you guys would've become roasted chicken." I said.

I could see Ella and Sapphire. They both were brutally hurt, but none of them were giving up. I've to help Sapphire. She can't do everything on her own. I reached the perfect spot, turned the truck at 180 degrees, with tires screeching, and opened the horizontal side of the truck.

I shouted, "Sapphire. Move aside."

She heard me and flew in the sky, while Ella jolted at the scene. All the laser beams she shot altogether to defeat Sapphire, had defeated her. The beams got reflected, hit her hard and she blasted away. She was down. I got off and ran to the battle area.

Sapphire and I approached her, still on our guard to check whether she was unconscious or not. As we were confirmed she was, we jumped in glee.

"Sapphire. Let's take her and you- you can create a magic jail and keep her trapped. And if she tries to communicate with that 'Drooller' monster, I'll handle her.", I said joyfully.

"Alright!", Sapphire transformed back into the bird, and continued, "Well, let's do it. But, I think she has the other 5 crystals."

"If you're right then let's keep her in the magical cage I was talking about and confront her once she's conscious.", I said, feeling victorious.

Then, I turned back to glance at Ella but saw that her sword was still moving. It had life or something.

Then, it struck me. Drogeler. It must be Drogeler's sword.

"Sapphie, look, the sword-" I couldn't complete as Sapphie was hit, and she screamed and fainted.

"What?", I gasped.

In fear and shock, I tried to run but was hit by the sword and everything became blank.

Chapter 38

Magic in My Veins

My head spun as I struggled to open my eyes, the effort feeling like I was pushing against a heavyweight. Slowly, my surroundings came into focus, though nothing looked familiar. A wave of confusion swept over me—I had no idea where I was or how I got here. I tried to push myself up, but my arms trembled under the strain, and my legs felt like they'd forgotten how to move.

My vision remained blurry, the shapes around me shifting and blending, making it impossible to get my bearings. I sank back down, overwhelmed by weakness, my thoughts racing as I tried to piece together what had happened. As I was standing up, I realized my hands were tied with chains and I was behind bars. It was a Dungeon. I went near the bars only to see Ella joining all the crystals. My jaw dropped. No! This can't be happening. When I was hit by the sword and fainted, she must've taken the four jewels from my backpack. I've to stop her.

I shouted, "What are you doing? Leave them."

"Do you think I'll listen? It's over for you.", Ella spoke.

I looked back for Sapphire. She was there but in pain. I can't believe there's nothing I can do. Sapphire is the only one who can break out of these bars.

I approached Sapphire and said, "Is it the end? We'll not do anything?"

"I'm afraid not. She has zapped my powers, and I'm hurt right now. Although, I'm trying to recover."

I gave her a weak smile. I turned back to see Ella smirking.

"Boo-Boo Enid. You couldn't save the World."

I was at my breaking point, but there was no way to get out of the dungeon. I was furious, helpless, and devastated as I couldn't do anything to stop her. She was winning and I was watching her win.

Suddenly, the ground began to shake, growing stronger with each passing second. Cracks spread across the walls like jagged scars, and chunks of plaster and stone started to fall, filling the air with dust and noise.

Ella said, "Farewell."

She grabbed the joint crystal and left the shattering cave, leaving Sapphire and me behind.

I asked, huffing with anxiety, "Sapphire! What to do now?"

"I've got an idea.", she spoke in her feeble voice. "But don't ask for its explanation right now. I'll give it later."

I nodded and followed her instructions without question. She stood up and, to my surprise, told me to cut my skin.

Hesitantly, I did as she asked, watching as she did the same to herself. Then, she extended her hand and told me to mix our blood, her eyes steady and serious as if this act held some deep meaning.

She said, "You now have some magical powers. Use them to get us out."

I was awestruck and wanted to know how this happened, but I focused on getting us out. I moved my hands upwards and with a deep breath, I froze the rocks falling due to the cave collapsing. Then, I held Sapphire and teleported us outside, safely, with my newly born powers. We got out, and my eyes hunted for Ella. I spotted her getting to the shore.

I said, "Sapphie! Let's run to her while you give me the explanation about the magic thing that just happened."

"Right now?"

I nodded.

"Oh! Fine! I'll give it."

I raced towards Ella and, Sapphire started to explain, "Listen! You're my descendant."

"Pardon? Your descendant?", I gasped.

"I know, it sounds weird, but you're."

"How's that possible? You're a bird, or a cat, or a fish, or a dragon. The point is, you're a magical shapeshifting creature. So-"

"I know it's a truth, which can't be easily accepted."

"Scientifically speaking, humans are descendants of Apes. However, you're a magical creature."

"So what? I can also become a human."

"No way! Why didn't you become one?"

"I lost the ability."

"Woah! You're saying that so casually."

"Well, it's not a thing to worry about. But Ella running away is definitely a thing to worry about." Sapphire said.

I was zooming in to catch Ella. I've no idea why she was going to the shore. Then, it hit me like a train. Drogeler! Drogeler was banished to the Japan Trench, and judging the text on the billboards, we're in Japan. She's going to hand over the crystals to that monster. I must stop her.

I dashed and screamed, "If you have any ounce of shame, don't give the crystals to that creature."

She heard and turned to me. She swung her sword at me, and I got blasted away. The people around us got terrified and started to run. No matter what I say, she'll not listen to me. I've to take her by force. I got up again and tried to stop her. This time, I had a bit of magic within me.

She said, "Aye, magicless! Wanna fight me?"

"Magicless, you say."

With that, I forwarded my hand towards her and blasted her away. Her reaction was worth watching. She was dumbfounded.

"How- how did you-you do that?" she stuttered.

"That- that's a secret." I mimicked her.

She was fuming with fury, and I couldn't enjoy less. I ran towards her, and she prepared herself to fight me. I landed a kick on her face, but she dodged it with a backflip. We continued to try punches but both of us dodged all. Well, that's because both of us went together to martial arts classes in the evening when we were ten.

"Can't believe you took his side.", I exclaimed.

"Well, believe it then. We're gonna win."

"I won't let that happen."

Suddenly, we both made a distance. I could feel myself becoming weak, but I didn't stop there. I've to give my all. I started dashing towards her but she outsmarted me. She flipped back and fell in the sea, to give the crystals to Drogeler, while I stood there helpless. My magic isn't strong enough to go in the water and Sapphire is still recovering.

Chapter 39
Ella's POV

I fell into the sea, the cold water rushing over me, while Enid stood on the shore, frozen in shock. My head throbbed with pain—"Ugh!" I groaned, holding it as everything felt blurry.

Slowly, I started to regain my senses, the sound of the waves bringing me back to reality. The problem is that the monster Drogeler has brainwashed me and has made me his puppet. I'm not able to control myself. I sometimes get out of it and come back to the real Ella but his control is so strong that I'm always pushed back to that version of Ella who has betrayed her mother, her friend, and everyone else.

My head again throbbed with sharp pain and I was pulled back to the fake Ella.

I said, "Good thing I fell into the sea, outsmarting that world hero."

Then, I started to swim towards Drogeler. Suddenly, I stopped. I came back to my senses. Again! Why am I doing this?

My eyes are getting blurry due to the tears. I'm hurting my best friend. Why did I get tangled in this mess? Again, with a throbbing pain in my head, I zoomed back to the evil me.

I reached his mansion and said, "Drogeler Sir! (Drogeler brat, to be honest), I've brought them all."

"You joined all the crystals?", he spoke, with his voice heavy.

"Yes, sir (brat! I'm not able to say what I want to)."

"I'm so proud of you, Ella." He snatched the crystals and started chanting some spells.

Suddenly, the crystals again dismantled and circled Drogeler. He was laughing like a maniac. He stopped when the spell was over.

"Finally! Finally!" He yelled. "I've become the greatest of all. I'll finally get out of water and rule the land." he said, sounding victorious.

He started to swim to the shore. I can't imagine what'll happen to everyone's life, and I'm to blame. I followed Drogeler to the shore, only imagining the worst. I hope Enid finds a solution; unlike I destroyed everything.

Chapter 40

The Beast Unleashed

I couldn't believe she outsmarted me. But it wasn't a time to regret. It was time to take action.

I asked, "Sapphie! What to do now? She went to Drogeler, with crystals. I failed. I failed you and everyone else."

"You did everything in your power. Don't regret the past. See how you can change the future.", she replied.

I turned to the shore and realized the ground was slightly shaking. I'm sick of shaking earth. But what I saw, was a terrible sight. In the dim light of dusk, a towering beast emerged, its skin a patchwork of scaly, greenish-gray patches and raw, twisted scars.

It was Drogeler. All the ten crystals were circling him. I led the crystals to him. A single, small mistake of mine, in Spain, had cost me a lot today. Tears were about to roll down my eyes, but I controlled them. He was walking towards me taking heavy steps, followed by Ella. For some reason, I was glued to my position. I couldn't run.

Sapphire screamed, "Run Enid! What're you waiting for?"

I heard her, but I couldn't move a muscle.

"You're the girl who brought me the first 5 crystals. Aren't you?" he asked in his heavy voice.

I couldn't say anything; I couldn't breathe. Why was this happening?

"Ha-ha. I guess it means a yes. Such a good duo, you both are. You two brought 5 crystals each for me. It's amazing, isn't it?" He looked at me, then at Ella, and smirked.

"Alas! You won't be able to meet each other again." Ella's and my eyes widened.

"Ha-ha. Look at your legit reactions."

I didn't understand why Ella's expressions were changing. But I've no time to think about this nor to regret anything.

Then he asked, "Where's your creature friend? She must've helped you. Didn't she?"

He's talking about Sapphire. Do they know each other?

"You're no match for her, Drogeler." I exclaimed.

"Really? Good thing you initiated to make me laugh.", he said sarcastically.

People's screams were getting louder and louder. Many were recording the situation. Policemen, lifeguards, and military surrounded the area. Helicopters were flying over us.

One of the men said, "Both of the girls, get away from the area. It's dangerous."

Drogeler signaled Ella to blow them off, and she did as he instructed. All the people were surprised, but the army had no effect. Ella was about to blow another troop, but I created a shield.

"Not this time!", I exclaimed.

Ella's expression first turned to wrath then to hurt. I didn't understand why, and I would've melted away, but I remembered the moments she attacked me and told me that she had turned to Drogeler's side, even if it hurts me to think of it. Then, all the policemen pointed their guns at Drogeler, Ella, and even me!

"Do I look stupid to you? Why point at me? I'm protecting you!" I shouted in frustration.

"Leave this to the adults, kiddo." said the general.

"Kiddo?" I exclaimed. "This 'kiddo' has powers and only this 'kiddo' can stop this freakin' monster and this puppet 'kiddo'."

All of them looked at me with disgusting expressions. They must've got confused by too many 'kiddos'. I ignored them and created a magical ball of power and threw it at Drogeler with all my might.

To my surprise, it didn't affect him one bit. But did impact his mood. He started to roar so loudly, that he must've broken the record of the loudest. People's screams were added as well.

The army tried to control the situation but couldn't. Secondly, they all were glaring at me like I was the villain. Oh, please! Someone tell them the real story.

Then what I saw was unbelievable! Ella turned her head upwards, with a jolt, and said, "Stop it, Brat!"

She grabbed a crystal circling him and said, "Enid! Take this before he-"

Then she yanked again, and her eyes turned pure white then said, "Sorry Sir." and placed back the crystal.

I couldn't believe what she was just about to do.

"Enid, he's losing control over Ella.", Sapphire told me.

"Losing control?", I asked.

"Yes! He's controlling her. He brainwashed her."

"How do you know that?"

"Did you forget I'm a magical creature?"

"I-" I couldn't complete the sentence as Drogeler covered Ella's head with his big claw and zapped magic out of her, then threw her aside.

"Enid! He is Ronia's-"

He didn't let Ella finish and blasted her off. She fainted. She was going to give some information about this creature, but he didn't let her. Now, it's only Drogeler against me.

Chapter 41

Enid vs Drogeler

Sapphire said, "Enid! Even if I recover, I won't be able to face off against Drogeler. It's you, who'll do so. You've magic flowing in your veins. Even if the magic tree weakened after Fulhu's magic memory erasure, you still have magic within you. Everyone has magic within themselves."

Her words gave me hope to fight Drogeler and retrieve the crystals. I focused on myself and started to generate magic within me. It was working! I couldn't believe it was. Nor Drogeler could.

"You-you're just creating an illusion."

"Poor Drogeler is now so helpless without his puppet that he thinks he's seeing a mirage.", I said, sarcastically.

He twitched his face with wrath. Then he created a ball of fire and shot at me. I dodged it and hit him instead, with my newly born power. He was taken aback but didn't give up. He came dashing towards me with full force to blast me off. I was prepared for all his attacks now. We continued to fight till I was exhausted.

He was a magical creature, and I was just a mere human with newly born powers. Obviously, I will exhaust myself. However, I still fought with all my might.

But, I was at a disadvantage. People were panicking and Drogeler was generating more power through their fear. He is the monster who 'feeds on fear'.

"Run away, you all. Your fears are only making him stronger."

At this point, I was all out of breath, and he had the upper hand, making me blast away. Feeling too weak, I couldn't pick myself up. I just lay there and glanced at Ella's face.

Whenever I see her face, all those happy memories come flashing back, and always wanna make me cry. Why everything turned out like this? Why do I have to be this weak and negligible? Why? Tears were rolling out due to pain and hurt. I somehow managed to pick myself up only to see Drogeler using his gigantic hands, snatching a little girl away from her parents.

He said, "Enid! You either give away your powers or- you know it all."

I forced myself to get up.

"Enid! A girl's life is in danger. Pick yourself up otherwise, you'll never be able to forgive yourself." I told myself.

Drogeler smirked. That smirking creature! I limped towards him, thinking of how to free the girl. The girl was crying badly. Her screams were echoing and her parents were whining.

I had to save their daughter and hand her over to them safely. My mind came up with no solution except to obey Drogeler. Her life is more important than my powers.

I went forward and said, "You'll let the girl go in return for my powers. Deal?"

"Of course, Enid hero. A deal is a deal."

He has crossed the line, but I had no choice. He leaped forward to grab me when 'someone' lounged on his face, and he fell backward. I took the opportunity to free the girl from his grip. I handed the girl to her parents, and they thanked me tons. When I looked back to see who it was, I couldn't believe my eyes.

Chapter 42

The Young Girl

The sight I saw was beyond my imagination. It was the young girl from the legend; she was fighting Drogeler. But Ronia had killed her. In disbelief, I started to search for Sapphire.

"Sapphire! Sapphire! Where are you? A ghost is fighting. First Manik, now the young girl."

The girl said, "Can't believe you didn't recognize me, Enid!"

I froze, my heart skipping a beat. "W-what?" I stammered, turning to face her fully. My breath hitched. "I do recognize you. You're... you're the young girl from the legend!"

"Young girl! What a terrible nickname! It's Sapphire. Why did no one back then tell the legend writers my name?"

My jaw dropped as realization hit me like a thunderbolt. "Sa-Sapphire? You're... you're the *young girl?*"

"Oh! Yes, I am." She smiled calmly as if this was a casual truth and went back to fight Drogeler while I stood there utterly dumbfounded.

"You recharge yourself and think of getting back the crystals, although I'm working on it. Also, save some chips for me!" She winked.

The young girl was with me all this time! The young girl was Sapphire. I'll take time to digest that, until then, I'll focus on recharging myself. I sat down there and watched their fight. On the other side, people were recording us.

Sapphire said, "Hey reporters! Post it and write Italian Heroes are back." She gave a wink.

Oh, Sapphire!

My body ached but I stood up and started to generate magic. It was weaker than before, but I was able to produce it. The slow process is because of my injuries. Thanks to Hera, Ella, Drogeler, and the whole journey, to be honest.

Then, I glanced at the battlefield and saw that Sapphire was barely holding on, her movement slow and strained. She told me she has lost the ability to become a human. She has probably used all the magic from her recovery to transform into a human. Drogeler possessed her power- meaning the crystals.

Without much thinking, I dashed to the battlefield with the little magic I had and bombed Drogeler.

"You wanna die, kid?", his eyes glaring wildly at me.

In rage, he was about to grab me when Ella leaped forward and splashed a magical portion on Drogeler, causing burns all over his face.

He roared in pain and rage. He leapt his hand forward and smacked Ella. She was about to fall hard when I created a soft surface, but she had fainted again.

Chapter 43

Ella's Memories

The last thing I saw was Enid saving me from my fall. I feel terrible for hurting Enid. She's the one who gave me so many happy memories of my life. In return, I caused her damage. As I lay down, I remember those times when it was just the two of us in our world.

It takes me back to the time when we were returning from her Flamenco practice, she tripped in the middle of the road and hurt her ankle a bit.

Clumsy Enid!

She wasn't even wearing her Flamenco shoes that day.

How forgetful she was!

And the time when it was Spring, Enid forgot her chemistry notebook so we both dashed out of the school to get it. Instead, we got distracted and sat by the lake to enjoy the season. We almost got suspended for this.

Those were the times!

All this crystal chase has separated us and to some extent, I'm also to blame. That's because I believed his lies.

TWO MONTHS AGO

I was pacing around my room trying to memorize a chapter from biology. It was a normal day like any other. It was Saturday, and I was following my weekend routine, which was studying at that moment.

My window was open, inviting a gentle breeze and the sun's golden glow to make my room lively. But then, in a blink, a streak of lightning shot inside and struck my mirror. It didn't crack.

My heart raced as the room fell eerily silent. The lights began to flicker wildly, their steady hum replaced by an unsettling buzz until they burst into shards with a sharp, final pop. They shattered with a loud cracking sound and my eyes flew wide with shock and my heart leaped into my stomach.

The mirror remained untouched, unyielding to the chaos, but the lights shattered. How's that possible? Besides, there was no thunderstorm, and it was sunny outside.

How can a lightning bolt strike inside my room? Or is it that a thundercloud was hovering above my house? Obviously, not possible. With a heavy heart, I decided to go downstairs.

I rushed to my door, only to find it locked. Panic surged through me as I jiggled the handle, the sound echoing unnervingly in the silence. Desperate, I grabbed whatever I could find—pens, bobby pins, even a ruler—but no matter what I tried, it wouldn't budge.

My breaths grew shallow, my chest tightening as fear took hold. My mother wasn't home. That thought hit like a punch to the gut. I was alone. Completely alone.

Was someone in the house? My ears strained for any sound. A creak, a footstep—anything. Or was this some prank from Enid? No, this felt too real. My pulse pounded in my ears, drowning out my thoughts. What if I was imagining it?

Then a chilling voice came from behind, "You're not imagining it."

I froze, every muscle in my body locked up. A scream tore from my throat, my hands trembling violently as I forced myself to turn around. My heart plummeted. I turned back and there was someone in my mirror. Not someone, something!

What's happening?

My thoughts spiralled—was there an intruder in my house? No, this thing wasn't human. It wasn't wearing a disguise; it was something far worse. And yet, it was in my mirror, speaking to me.

This wasn't possible. It couldn't be possible. But I realized the impossible had become terrifyingly real.

"Hey! Finally, I saw a human after thousands of years."

I screamed, though my voice barely leaping from my throat, "Thousand years? Who are you? No! What are you?"

"That's a harsh question. You humans were never nice.", he replied in a heavy voice.

"Why? Aren't you a human? Wait! Why am I asking this? Simple answer. You aren't a human because if you were, you wouldn't look like a dinosaur.", I said.

I thought that thing would get offended and probably leave me thinking that I'm courageous or he couldn't harm me (Though I'm not brave. I might've faced some bullies but not dinosaurs). To my surprise, it started laughing softly.

"I'm Drogeler. I am a magical creature who wants you to find some magical crystals that'll set me free so that I can save the world from dissolving into eternal darkness. I know it's hard to believe what I'm saying. Magic. Magical creature. Eternal darkness. These are terms that you humans only hear in fairy tales. That's why I'm providing you with help through books. These have plenty of knowledge that will allow you to trust magic and find those crystals for me. I know you'll disagree but you've to do it otherwise this planet will shatter and fall into doom. The choice is yours. Become a hero or become a traitor." Saying that he disappeared leaving me completely awestruck.

Of course, now I understand that he spelled back then so that I'll believe his fake sweet world-saving speech to help him set free. And what happened?

Obviously, I believed him. When I had questions, he always answered them softly like he was the good guy. I asked a lot of questions after he gave his fake sweet speech on how the crystals would affect the world, how he was trapped, how would I get them, what things should I work on, does anyone else know it, and many more questions.

I was definitely not going to blindly believe him. He answered them all swiftly and so he gained my trust. Even though, I felt something fishy about him I carried on with my research work.

Then, one day, while I was working on finding the crystals and he was there in my mirror guiding me, a question arose in my mind.

I asked him, "What'll you do with the crystals?"

"Possess their powers and use them for the greater good to protect the world.", He replied calmly.

"How exactly?" I questioned back.

He raised his eyebrows, his sinister smile growing colder. It was easier for him to make a new lie but instead, he chose to gain complete control of me so that I don't ever question him again and just obey him. And when he did, I lost myself.

Chapter 44

Enid's Memories

Ella fainted while protecting me. All these recent actions of hers make me believe that she was not entirely responsible for this mess. She was the closest and the only friend I ever had. Whenever she was around me, I felt courageous and less scared, even the bullies didn't disturb me.

I remember when we first met on the beach, and we were playing suddenly many fireflies surrounded us. Ella was surprised stating that I had a great talent. But I had no idea how they were present there. But now I know, it was me who created them. I created them through magic. Because I had been Sapphire's descendent. Then, I was shocked myself but played along cuz' I was a kid back then who didn't care about reason.

I remember, when we were nine, she took me to her painting class and, she painted so beautifully and gracefully. Her painting classes were on Sundays. After the day I went to her painting class, I visited her often. Once she even painted both of us. I still have that painting, framed in my room. She even painted our principal but with a moustache and two antennas. That painting was hilarious.

We were thinking of gifting it to our principal on her birthday under an anonymous name but later dropped our plan as we didn't want to be in trouble.

We used to chat, laugh, eat, and enjoy every day. She lit up a light in my darkness of life. Friends like her are rare and people who've them are lucky. I considered myself lucky too, as I had a friend like Ella. She is the one who protected me from the bullies and always gave me valour.

Once, on a field trip, somebody bullied me, so she formulated a plan. She decided to sneak into their camps and apply glue to their sleeping bags. And so, we did. We barely escaped though. What a prank it was! Their reaction was worth watching. After that, we took a walk in the lap of nature, enjoying ourselves as always.

I miss the days when we were carefree, living in the joy of each moment and turning them into memories worth cherishing. Back then, it felt like nothing could come between us. But now, this relentless chase for the crystals and the chaos with Drogeler have created a distance I never thought possible.

It's as if the weight of it all has pulled us into separate worlds.

Chapter 45
Beginning of the End

Drogeler was outraging and attacking us intensely.

"You don't know. Your partner killed my mother.", he screamed.

"M-mother?", I asked.

Sapphire's face turned pale.

"Oh yes. Ronia, the most powerful witch in the world. Your 'sapphie' killed her. No one was a match for her UNTIL she came."

My jaw dropped. He's Ronia's son?

He continued, "My mom had two powers left before dying, so she used one of them to kill your 'sapphie' but instead she survived. And the other she transferred to me, and I became an immortal fear-feeding monster to follow my mother's prophecy."

"Your mother's prophecy!? To kill people heartlessly or to live on people's fear or disrupt the peace of the world? That's your prophecy." Sapphire screamed.

In this journey, I never saw her snapping until now.

"Of course. That's the prophecy and I'm gonna take revenge, by using your power. Ha-ha-ha." Drogeler gave an evil laugh.

Sapphire and I glanced at each other and understood the signal. We had to take away the crystals from him as soon as possible. Sapphire and I sprang into action. We threw magical balls of fire, wind, water, ice, and whatnot. Then Sapphire brought her wrists together, kept her palms apart, and said, "Devil's eye!", pointing at Drogeler.

"Devil's eyes! That's the symbol of South Africa!", I exclaimed.

"And that's the power of Hypnotism."

Then, Sapphire struck him with a magical blast and 3 crystals were out of his control.

"Freakin' cool.", I said, admiring the powers of the lost crystals.

"Every symbol represents a power. Now it's time for 'Water Wave'. " Sapphire told me.

Water waves started to pour out from her hands and suffocated Drogeler. One more crystal out from his seal. 6 more to go.

"Enid! I want you to make him angry.", Sapphire ordered.

"Isn't he angry enough!"

"Not for my plan."

I nodded reluctantly and said to Drogeler, "Hey whining Droogler! Catch me if you can."

With that, I started spinning around him. He got dizzy and furious. "Don't play with me, kid."

"That's the last straw. After this, you won't ever call me kid."

Saying that I landed a huge punch on his nose. Then, he roared, breaking his own record. At this time, he was out of control due to his outburst and Sapphie took advantage of this. She doubled the size of her palm and grabbed all the crystals in one go. I couldn't have been any happier.

"Go Sapphie!"

However, my excitement didn't last for long as Drogeler, coming back to his senses but still furious, grabbed Sapphire hard and she dropped all the crystals from her grip on the ground. I dashed in their direction to pick them up before they got into the hands of Drogeler. However, a person near the area started to pick them up.

The person was Ella.

Chapter 46

Possession

Ella had woken up and now was collecting the crystals.

I wanted to say-Stop it, traitor. But something inside me didn't allow me to do so.

She picked them up and said, "Enid! Catch and possess them."

I couldn't believe it—she was actually giving the crystals to me! Her hand trembled as she held them out, but just as I reached for them, Drogeler's influence took over. His dark command rang out, freezing her in place. Her eyes filled with tears as she pulled back, and my heart sank.

"No! Not again!", she spoke, as if she was in sharp pain.

I dashed towards her.

"Ella! Give me the crystals," demanded Drogeler.

"No, Ella! You won't. Hand them over to me.", I spoke.

Suddenly, she started to scream intensely. She didn't give the crystals to Drogeler or me as she was resisting Drogeler's control.

Drogeler noticed this in an instant and commanded, "Ella. You possess them."

"What?!" Sapphire, Ella, and I exclaimed altogether.

"No-no I won't." Ella screamed helplessly.

"Ella! Look at me. You can control yourself.", I spoke, with my voice trembling.

I encouraged her with every word I could muster, and she fought with all her strength. Suddenly, she began chanting the spell, her voice trembling as the crystals responded. She resisted with everything she had, tears streaming down both our faces. Drogeler's maniacal laughter filled the air, mocking her struggle. I clenched my fists, teeth gritting in frustration. But then, a spark of hope arose- Ella seemed to be gaining control.

"Ella. You're the one who always gave me courage. You're the one who made me stronger. Because of your motivation, I was able to find the five crystals. Without the courage you gave me all these years, I wouldn't have even started the journey.", I screamed and spoke the sentence at 2x speed.

She looked at me with a weak smile and said, "Will you be able to forgive me, someday?"

"Not someday, today." I smiled and she smiled back.

Then, she screamed, getting out of Drogeler's control and terminated the possession of the red crystals.

"Enid! You possess the crystals. You're the worthy holder of them.", Ella spoke as she fell on the ground and I held her gently.

"What?! No, I can't. I-"

"I know you'll protest. But, I know you have the heart of a warrior. You're brave, confident, and have all the traits a power keeper needs. These crystals are meant for you." Ella said, looking at me with determination.

"She's right, Enid. You're a worthy power holder.", Sapphire spoke from behind.

Chapter 47

The Worthy Holder

I took a deep breath. I couldn't believe that I was going to possess these powerful artifacts. But it's not a time for jaw-dropping. I took the crystals from Ella. From far away, Drogeler was shouting, "No! No!"

Then, he started to dash towards us, but Sapphire stopped him.

She said, "I'll keep him at bay. You chant the spell."

I chanted, "Crystallum Possidere."

Then the ten crystals began to circle me, and a surge of energy shot through my veins. They twirled and sparkled, coming together as one, and I could feel the immense power of their magic flooding within me.

All the magic inside me burst. It was like nothing I'd ever experienced—raw, electrifying, and unstoppable. My outfit shimmered and transformed, taking on a new, dazzling form, while my hair flowed with radiant energy. I felt a wave of power unlike anything before, as if the very core of the crystals had merged with my soul. I felt unstoppable now.

Drogeler shouted, "Nooooo!!"

This time, it was my turn to smirk at him.

"Poor Drogeler. Not able to live up to his mummy's prophecy."

He completely lost control. His eyes burned with fury as he charged at me, launching attacks that, at first, seemed powerful. But as they came toward me, I barely flinched—his strikes were nothing. I felt the magic inside me roar to life.

With a swift motion, I summoned a massive wave of water, swirling it around me like a shield. At the same time, I invoked the Devil's Eye, sending a hypnotic wave towards him. His movements slowed down; his mind clouded as I locked his gaze.

With the perfect opportunity, I struck him—slamming my fist into his chest with all my strength. To my shock, he began to disintegrate, his form breaking apart, fading like dust in the wind.

But it wasn't over. He snapped back to reality, fury flashing in his eyes. His body reformed, and he surged at me again, now desperate, attacking with reckless abandon. I didn't hesitate. Lightning surged from my hands, crackling through the air, striking him with precision.

Each bolt hit harder than the last, and I could see his frustration growing. He must've realized what I already knew; his power was fading. His once overwhelming strength was slipping through his fingers. This was my moment, my chance to end it all.

I lifted my hands to form a dragon out of fire and said, "Go Drakon! Wrap him."

She followed my instructions and wrapped him, causing burns on his scales. He screamed in agony, his shouts filled with desperation as his body twisted with each failed attempt to strike me down. The crowd watched, recording every moment of the battle. I stood there firmly boosted with energy.

I consumed back the dragon after his job was done and said, "Gave up already?"

He looked at me with his yellow, weak eyes and then he fell. I didn't expect that to happen. Not really. Suddenly, all the people started cheering, applauding, and hooding in joy and relief.

A wave of relaxation surged over me because this battle had been too heavy on me. I was exhausted due to the battle. I turned around to face the crowd and Ella. She smiled at me, and I realized everything had finally turned back to normal. I looked around for Sapphire.

She must be worn out as well, perhaps more than me because she had lost the ability to become a human but had to become one to assist me in facing that wretched monster.

Suddenly Ella and many other people shouted, "Look behind you!"

I turned my head in a hurry and saw Drogeler rising. Then he was approaching Sapphire, so I alerted her, "Move away, Sapphire!"

But it was too late, and he had already scratched her horribly. She was on the floor shedding blood. I dashed towards her and tears rolled out of my eyes.

"Sapphire! Sapphire! NO! NO! Someone call an ambulance."

I was done with him. My blood burned with fury, each second more unbearable than the last. How dare he hurt Sapphire? My hands shook with rage as I stepped forward, my eyes locked onto him.

"That's enough of you!" I screamed my voice a roar of pure, unrelenting fury.

Chapter 48

Triumph of Peace

I charged at him, my feet pounding against the ground, my body fueled by rage. Each step brought me closer, and as I reached him, I struck him—again and again—each more powerful than the last.

I unleashed everything I had. Water waves crashed against him, slamming him with force. The Devil's Eye paralyzed him for a split second, leaving him vulnerable. Lightning bolts crackled from my hands, searing his scales with relentless intensity. I called upon fire, sending flames that scorched everything in their path.

With a roar, I summoned the dragon's power, its fierce energy coiling around me, crashing into him with unstoppable force.

I felt him weaken under each blow. His body stumbled, his movements growing more sluggish as my attacks drained him. But I wasn't done. My fury surged, driving me forward. I wasn't going to stop until he paid for what he did to Sapphire.

"You've done enough, you monster!" I screamed, my teeth gritting in fury.

I continued striking, my powers tearing through his defences. His form began to falter, pieces of him disintegrating with every hit. Finally, I looked up, and to my shock, he was nothing but a pile of disintegrating ashes. His body crumbled, his lower half vanishing into nothingness.

I took a step back, breathing heavily, my body trembling with exhaustion. The battle was over.

I turned to the crowd, signalling them with a raised hand. It was finished. The war had ended, and this time, the cheers that erupted around me were louder, stronger, and more triumphant than ever before.

Ella came rushing toward me, her face streaked with tears and wrapped her arms around me. Before I knew it, my tears spilled over, matching hers. We held onto each other like we were afraid to let go.

"I'm so sorry, I'm so sorry," she sobbed, over and over, her voice cracking with guilt.

"It's okay," I whispered. "I forgive you. I always will."

Then, I went to check Sapphire, and she was still breathing.

"You're alive.", I said, my voice shaking.

"Of course, I am. How would I miss the victory party, which'll be full of chips?" She winked and continued, "You are a worthy power keeper, even more than I ever was."

Happy tears started to roll down from my eyes. Now, she won't be able to turn back to a human. But it doesn't matter. As long as she's there, I'm happy. I'm glad that everything has turned back to normal.

Chapter 49

Reunion

Well, what happened after that?

We all returned to our normal life. Ella and I returned to Milan and found our mothers sitting together, having coffee, with pale faces, because they must be worried sick as both of us disappeared without a warning.

We both developed courage and said, "Hello, mom."

They both gasped, ran towards us, and hugged us both tightly.

Then Mrs. Rossi said, "Why were you two on the news? How did you hack the news channel? How did you do such great animations? Do you think it's a toy?"

Ella and I glanced at each other and burst into laughter.

Mrs. Rossi glared at us and then I spoke, "That was no animation. We were fighting."

I sparked my hand and both of their mouths fell open.

My mother said, "This isn't a time for magic tricks."

After that, we sat in the backyard and shared our sides of the story. How Ella was manipulated to obey Drogeler and how she was later brainwashed when she tried to stop him.

Whereas I explained how I got hold of Ella's book and the magical potions, to start the journey of finding the ten crystals of the legend. My mother gasped at the revelation that the story she used to narrate to me when I was little was true.

I told them how I sneaked into the memorial of South Africa, got trapped in Indonesia, went underwater and fought Manik (a ghost) in Maldives, got a chance to show my dance skills but then got robbed by the dancers in Spain and how I fought an enormous dragon in Greece. And how can I miss the final battle I had with Drogeler?

Both were stunned and well, they didn't scold us, as we did such a great job, in saving the world. I also introduced them to Sapphire. My mother screamed but Mrs. Rossi squealed. But this was only the beginning of explaining our stories.

We had to tell our stories to our neighbours, and relatives, then to the world via interviewers. We both attended so many shows.

I said, "Mama Mia! We've become celebrities."

Ella replied, "Oh yes! I always had the thought that one day, you and me, at the runway, with paparazzi chasing us and-"

"You and your delulu."

"You're much more delulu than me, sister."

Later, when we returned to school, all those who were our bullies wanted to be friends with us. Both of us became the cool kids.

After that, people labelled us as 'heroes'. I liked the idea. But, unfortunately, my neighbours labelled me as an engineer.

One said, "Enid dear! My fridge stopped working. Can you use your powers to cool it?"

Another one said, "Enid! You're my lifesaver! Please fix my microwave."

While, my mother said, "Use your heat to help me cook. The gas stove stopped working."

Other time she said, "Enid! Use your water power to wash the dishes. The water isn't gonna come till 2 hours."

I'm a superhero, not a person who'll go to people's houses and fix their fridges, and microwaves, wash dishes, or light a gas stove in my own house.

Alas!

However, I'm not complaining. I'm really happy in fact; peace has remained in its place, and I didn't let Drogeler win. As I look back on those moments now, I realize that what felt like an overwhelming battle at the time was, in fact, something much greater. It wasn't just a struggle; it was an extraordinary adventure that shaped me in ways I couldn't have imagined.

Chapter 50

Moments of Bliss

Ella and I headed to her house to help her clean her room, as I told you earlier, her room was a big mess. I said, "You take the bed and the window area. I'll do your desk till then."

"Roger."

As I was cleaning her desk, I came across a paper with some magic happening in it.

I asked, "What's this?"

"Oh, that. It's my exam paper. I was changing my marks. He-he."

I smacked her head.

"Sorry, I was under the control of that monster."

We both laughed.

AFTER ONE YEAR

It's been a year since the Drogeler incident. I'm in 12th grade now.

So far so good.

Ella is going to pursue engineering in the future. At least, people will stop making me their engineer. Good riddance. Sapphire has also recovered, and she is now able to shape-shift into different animals. Mom and Sapphire have become such good friends.

Mom is like, "Sapphire is such a cutie."

"You think that because you weren't on the journey with her. She's a chatterbox who's insanely obsessed with chips.", I exclaimed.

"That's the thing I love about her."

Then, they both burst into laughter, and I slipped away to let them have their moment. After all the incidents, I changed. I became a better version of myself.

Ella and I spend our evenings together, following our old traditions. We go on walks, to the parks or stay at each other's houses. Today, Ella will hang out at my house.

As usual, we had loads of fun and later rested for a while.

Then, Ella asked me a question, "Hey, E. Anything planned to do next?"

I understood what she was talking about.

"Oh yes! I do have something in mind." I smiled.

THE END.

Epilogue

I was dancing with my plants to the song 'Flowers'.

I started to sing, "I-can-buy-myself-flowers. Write-my-name-in-the-sand. Talk-to-myself-for-hours. Saying-things-you-don't-understand. That's-all-the-song-I-knowwwwww."

I finished the song on a long note, twirled, and ended my performance. When I opened my eyes, I fell in shock upon seeing a lady in front of me.

She spoke, "Hello there! Great dancer you are. Not to mention your singing skills."

"I'll take that as a compliment. Wait a minute! Who are you, and how did you enter my house? This is trespassing. No one can enter my house. I mean, they can, but they won't be able to as the door is covered in ivy vines." I exclaimed.

"Like this.", she said, sparking her hand and, she disappeared. I looked sideways, but she was gone. Then someone tapped my shoulder from behind and I turned around to look only to scream and fall again. It was the same lady.

"Like this.", she repeated.

She's cool but... she frightened me.

"Oh! Nice! You didn't have to scare me like that. Anyway, I guess you've powers like me." I said, catching my breath.

"Yes, Zoe. That's why I'm here. With an offer." She replied.

"What offer?" I asked, curious.

"To become a defender."

"A defender?"

"Yes. A defender of the World."

Quotes

"When you hear the call of adventure, make sure that HOPE catches you first."

— Enid

"FIGHT LIKE A NINJA!"

— Sapphire

"Overcome your Phobia. You can do anything you want if your willpower is strong."

— Sapphire

"Become the Queen of Water and defeat that phobia of yours."

— Sapphire

"Let's not lose hope and keep moving forward."

— Enid

*"No matter how many phobias I've,
I'll still rise and bring my inner bravery to life."*

- Enid

*"You've two choices- If you're scared, so go
and hide, but if you're bold and eager to save everyone,
then confront the villain."*

- Sapphire

"Everyone has magic within themselves."

- Sapphire.

Which Symbol Do You Represent?

1. Devil's Eye (South Africa)- Wants to open the world's closed eyes.

2. Breeze of Freedom (Indonesia)- Wants to be completely free and independent.

3. Water Wave (Maldives)- Loves oceans and beaches.

4. The Star (Spain)- Wants to be unique and stand out.

5. The Dragon (Greece)- Wants to be brave, majestic, strong, and confident.

Symbols that were not mentioned (As they were solved and found by Ella)

1. Fire of your desire (Brazil)- Working hard for your desire to be fulfilled.

2. Lightning bolt (Thailand)- The one who lights up the dark.

3. Wings of unity (UK)- Wants to fly high and succeed in life.

4. Mirrored Triangle (Costa Rica)- Lives in one's imagination.

5. Sound wave (USA)- Loves Music and feels it move in one's veins

www.ingramcontent.com/pod-product-compliance
Lightning Source LLC
LaVergne TN
LVHW041844070526
838199LV00045BA/1431